THE LORD OF THE HALLOWS

CHRISTIAN S

J. K. ROV

CW01080566

MES IN

ER

THE LORD OF THE HALLOWS

CHRISTIAN SYMBOLISM AND THEMES IN
J. K. ROWLING'S HARRY POTTER

DENISE ROPER

Outskirts Press, Inc.
Denver, Colorado

Dedication

To my mother, Aleta, who always believed in me.

To Tina, who first introduced me to the Boy Who Lived.

An to Merril, Dorothy, Karl, and Cecile, because the ones who love us never truly leave us.

The Lord of the Hallows
Christian Symbolism and Themes in J. K. Rowling's Harry Potter
All Rights Reserved.
Copyright © 2009 Denise Roper
v3.0

Outskirts Press, Inc.
http://www.outskirtspress.com

ISBN: 978-1-4327-4112-9

Library of Congress Control Number: 2009927104

Outskirts Press and the "OP" logo are trademarks belonging to Outskirts Press, Inc.

PRINTED IN THE UNITED STATES OF AMERICA

Contents

Abbreviations Used in This Book

The Harry Potter books by J. K. Rowling
SS *Harry Potter and the Sorcerer's Stone* (*Harry Potter and the Philosopher's Stone*)
CS *Harry Potter and the Chamber of Secrets*
PA *Harry Potter and the Prisoner of Azkaban*
GF *Harry Potter and the Goblet of Fire*
OP *Harry Potter and the Order of the Phoenix*
HBP *Harry Potter and the Half-Blood Prince*
DH *Harry Potter and the Deathly Hallows*
TBB *Tales of Beedle the Bard*
Works by J. R. R. Tolkien:
LOTR *The Lord of the Rings* (one volume hardcover edition)
Hobbit refers to *The Hobbit*
Letters refers to *The Letters of J. R. R. Tolkien* edited by Humphrey Carpenter
The essay "On Fairy Stories" can be found on pages 33-99 of *The Tolkien Reader*.

Bible quotations:

NRSV *New Revised Standard Version: Catholic Edition*

KJV *King James Version*

For all other quotations, please refer to list of Works Cited.

1

Sneaking Past the Watchful Dragons

What is the secret of the world-wide popularity of J. K. Rowling's *Harry Potter* novels? This is the question that many critics, scholars, and fans have been trying to answer for more than a decade. I believe that one reason for the novels' success can be found in their hidden meaning. The Christian symbolism and imagery used by Rowling is the key to unlocking the secrets of this seven book series. J. K. Rowling is a Christian fantasy novelist following in the tradition of C. S. Lewis and J. R. R. Tolkien.

    C. S. Lewis was one of the greatest Christian apologists and theologians of the 20th Century as well as being the author of the beloved seven volume fantasy *The Chronicles of Narnia*. Lewis was a great lover of fairy tales. The phrase "baptism of the imagination" was coined by Lewis to describe how such fairy stories could prepare a person's mind to be open to the truths of Christianity. In a letter he penned in 1939, Lewis wrote "…any amount of theology can now be smuggled into people's minds under cover of romance without their knowing it." Lewis referred to "stealing past the watchful dragons" in the essay "Sometimes Fairy Stories May Say Best What's to Be Said."

> Why did one find it so hard to feel as one ought to feel about God or about the sufferings of Christ? I thought the chief reason was that one was told one ought to....But supposing that by casting all these things into an imaginary world, stripping them of their stained-glass and Sunday school associations, one could make them for the first time appear in their real potency? Could one not steal past those watchful dragons? I thought one could. (*On Stories* 47)

Lewis did indeed "steal past the watchful dragons" of secularism in his *Chronicles of Narnia* novels. He effectively smuggled Christian morality, symbolism, and a certain amount of allegory into that popular series of children's fantasy novels, with many of his readers both young and old being unaware of the fact that they were being taught religious truths while being entertained.

Lewis had been an atheist for a number of years before experiencing a conversion to the Christian religion. This conversion was due in part to the influence of two of his friends: Hugo Dyson and J. R. R. Tolkien.

J. R. R. Tolkien, a devout Catholic Christian, believed that the creation of a fantasy world such as his own Middle-Earth is a kind of "sub-creation" which imitates God's creation of our own world. Ronald Tolkien called his own epic fantasy, *The Lord of the Rings*, "a fundamentally religious and Catholic work; unconsciously so at first, but consciously in the revision." He goes on to say:

SNEAKING PAST THE WATCHFUL DRAGONS

That is why I have not put in, or have cut out, practically all references to anything like "religion," to cults and practices, in the imaginary world. For the religious element is absorbed into the story and the symbolism. (*Letters* 172)

Though there seems to be little or no outward trappings of organized religion in Tolkien's fictional world of hobbits, wizards, and elves, the Christian symbolism and imagery used by the author, along with the morality that is embedded in the text gives much support to Tolkien's claim that *The Lord of the Rings* is indeed a fundamentally Christian story.

J. K. Rowling gave her readers clues that she was following the path of Lewis and Tolkien when she gave an interview with the *Vancouver Sun* in the year 2000. The journalist asked "Are you a Christian?" and Rowling's response was:

"Yes, I am. Which seems to offend the religious right far worse than if I said I thought there was no God. Every time I've been asked if I believe in God, I've said *yes*, because I do, but no one ever really has gone any more deeply into it than that, and I have to say that does suit me, because if I talk too freely about that I think the intelligent reader, whether 10 or 60, will be able to guess what is coming in the books." (Wyman)

In a subsequent interview, Rowling told the journalist with questions about her faith to come back after the seventh book, and that, if he had read it, he wouldn't have to come back because his questions would be answered. (Solomon)

There is also evidence that in addition to being a Christian writer, J. K. Rowling is a great admirer of the creators of both Narnia and

Middle-earth. Rowling has said of Lewis and Tolkien, "I've read both of them—both of them were geniuses. I'm immensely flattered to be compared to them [...]" (Lydon). In the BBC Red Nose Day Chat of 2001, Rowling was asked, "Did you read the Narnia books as a child?" Her response was, "Yes I did and I liked them, though all the Christian symbolism utterly escaped me. It was only when I re-read them later in life that it struck me forcibly." Rowling has claimed to enjoy Lewis's fiction even as an adult: "Even now, if I was in a room with one of the Narnia books I would pick it up like a shot and re-read it." (De Bertodano 3)

Since the late 1990's, Rowling's fiction has been favorably compared to Lewis's, but after the release of *Harry Potter and the Deathly Hallows*, comparisons with *The Lord of the Rings* were also inevitable. Tolkien scholar Joseph Pearce identifies the religious elements in *The Lord of the Rings* as follows:

> In general terms the religious element falls into three distinct but inter-related areas: the sacrifice which accompanies the selfless exercise of free will; the intrinsic conflict between good and evil; and the perennial question of time and eternity, particularly in relation to life and death. (Pearce 111)

From the beginning of the series it has been evident that Rowling's novels have the same religious themes as Tolkien's. These themes will be examined farther in chapter three. But first will examine some of the more obvious similarities between Tolkien's and Rowling's fantastic worlds in the next chapter.

2

Harry and the Hobbits

When J. K. Rowling was asked specifically how much her writing was influenced by Tolkien, she responded:

> Hard to say. I didn't read *The Hobbit* until after the first Harry Potter book was written, though I read *The Lord of the Rings* when I was nineteen. I think, setting aside the obvious fact that we both use myth and legend, that the similarities are fairly superficial. Tolkien created a whole new mythology, which I would never claim to have done. On the other hand, I think I have better jokes.—J. K. Rowling on October 16, 2000.

In this chapter we will take a closer look at those "fairly superficial" similarities between Rowling and Tolkien. One indication of Tolkien's influence on Rowling's work can be found in the frequent use of Middle-earth inspired names in the wizarding world. Butterbeer is a non-intoxicating drink favored by Hogwarts students. In *The Lord of the Rings,* Barliman Butterbur is the innkeeper at the Prancing Pony in Bree, a town inhabited by both humans and hobbits. The Prancing Pony is known for its excellent beer. "Longbottom Leaf" may sound like one of Neville Longbottom's herbology assignments, but in Middle-earth, Longbottom Leaf is a type of pipe-weed grown in the Southfarthing of the Shire.

Hobbit-like names are everywhere in Harry's world. There is an Auror named Proudfoot mentioned by Tonks. (HBP 158) Proudfoot is also the surname of a family of Shire hobbits related to Bilbo Baggins by marriage. (LOTR 28) There is also the familiar surname of the hobbit family named Puddifoot from the Eastfarthing. The Puddifoots of Stock were house-dwelling hobbits that lived near Farmer Maggot. (LOTR 90) One can't help but wonder if they are related to the owner of Madame Puddifoot's Tea Shop, a place where Harry and Cho Chang went on a date in book five. An inspection of the hobbit family trees in the appendix of *The Lord of the Rings* reveals Baggins family members named Mungo, Pansy, Lily, and Myrtle. The Took family has a member named Hugo, and the Brandybuck family includes hobbits named Rose, Rufus, and Burrows. Still not convinced? The famous magical historian Bathilda Bagshot lived near Harry's parents in the town of Godric's Hollow. Please note that Sam Gamgee's father, "The Gaffer," lives at Number 3 Bagshot Row in Hobbiton. Frodo's old acquaintance, Farmer Maggot, owns a dog named Fang, and so does Harry's friend Hagrid.

Brave sidekicks Sam Gamgee and Ron Weasley both end up marrying their sweethearts and having families that include a female named "Rose." Rose Cotton became Sam's wife, and among their many children was a daughter also named Rose. Likewise, Hermione Granger became Ron's wife and they also had a daughter named Rose and a son named Hugo.

HARRY AND THE HOBBITS

There are similarities in the nomenclature of villains as well. Both *The Lord of the Rings* and *Harry Potter* have cowardly and treacherous traitors with similar names: Wormtongue and Wormtail. And of course, Voldemort was not the first "Dark Lord" in fantasy literature. The Dark Lord was a title previously reserved for Sauron the Great, Lord of the Rings and Ruler of Mordor. (LOTR 49-50) Boromir, the eldest son of the Steward of Gondor, would not say the name of Sauron aloud: "I have heard of the Great Ring of him that we do not name." (LOTR 237) Boromir's younger brother Faramir later refers to Sauron as "he whom we do not name." (LOTR 656) The sons of the Steward of Gondor have something in common with most of the wizards in Harry's world: they will not say the Dark Lord's name aloud, referring to Voldemort as "He-Who-Must-Not-Be-Named."

Other similarities include the references to "Goblin Wars" (*Hobbit* 49) and the numerous mentions of "Goblin Rebellions" in Professor Binns' History of Magic class. Hogwarts students can also study Ancient Runes. Hermione, like Bilbo Baggins, can decipher the mysterious runes, and that skill comes in handy when Bilbo is trying to decipher a map to the dragon Smaug's treasure or when Hermione is translating *The Tales of Beedle the Bard*.

Both Middle-earth and the wizarding world are populated with deadly monsters: trolls, giant spiders, and fire-breathing dragons, just to name a few.

Bilbo had a frightening encounter with three hungry trolls in *The Hobbit*. The Fellowship's battle with the cave troll in the Mines of Moria was one of the most exciting action sequences in Peter Jackson's film adaptation of the first part of *The Lord of the Rings*. In this sequence (as in Harry, Ron, and Hermione's battle with the mountain troll in *Harry Potter and the Sorcerer's Stone)* teamwork and courage were required to defeat the monster.

Both Tolkien and Rowling have claimed that their fictional giant spiders were manifestations of their own arachnophobia. Ronald Weasley and the author who created him are both terrified of spiders. (Please note that John Ronald Reuel Tolkien was usually called "Ron" or "Ronald" by his friends and family.) Aragog's name even sounds like it could belong to Shelob's family tree.

In Bilbo Baggins' first venture into Smaug's lair, he stole a two-handled cup from the dragon's hoard. Harry, Ron, and Hermione also took a valuable cup from a treasure room guarded by a dragon when they took the Cup of Hufflepuff from the bank vault of Bellatrix Lestrange in *Harry Potter and the Deathly Hallows*. Both Smaug and the Gringott's dragon created mayhem after the theft was discovered. When Bilbo first met Smaug, he thought the dragon was asleep; this was a dangerous mistake.

> "Never laugh at live dragons, Bilbo you fool!" he said to himself, and it became a favourite saying of his later, and passed into a proverb. (*Hobbit* 204)

Bilbo's "proverb" might very well be the precursor to the Hogwarts school motto: *Never tickle a sleeping dragon*. Prepare to sneak past the watchful dragons identified by C. S. Lewis in the next chapter, which will examine Christian themes in the *Harry Potter* series.

3

Christian Themes in the Story of Harry Potter

In the *Harry Potter* novels, there are a number of Christian themes, including free will, life after death, the immortality of the soul, and the power of love and self-sacrifice. The importance of loyalty and friendship is also given consideration in this discussion.

it is not our abilities that make us who we truly our, it is our choices

1. Free Will

The notion that human beings determine their own salvation or demise by the choices they make in this life can be found in the Old Testament.

> It was he who created humankind in the beginning, and he left them in the power of their own free choice. If you choose, you can keep the commandments, and to act faithfully is a matter of your own choice. He has placed before you fire and water; stretch out your hand for whichever you

choose. Before each person are life and death, and whichever one chooses will be given. (Sirach 15: 14-17 NRSV; see also Deuteronomy 30: 15-20)

In the Christian religion, human beings have been given knowledge of the difference between good and evil, and each person must choose between the two throughout his or her lifetime. This task has been placed before mankind since the days of Adam and Eve in the Garden of Eden.

The Sorting Hat in *Harry Potter and the Sorcerer's Stone* wanted to put Harry in Slytherin, a house associated with Dark Wizards. The Sorting Hat told him he could be great there, but Harry's repeated denial of the Sorting Hat's promptings caused the hat to put him in Gryffindor. (SS 121)

> "It only put me in Gryffindor," said Harry in a defeated voice, "because I asked not to go in Slytherin…."
>
> "*Exactly*," said Dumbledore, beaming once more. "Which makes you *very different* from Tom Riddle. It is our choices, Harry, that show who we truly are far more than our abilities." (CS 333)

This last statement from Dumbledore sums up the theme of the second novel, and one of the most important themes of the entire series. The values of the fallen world in which we live are the same as the qualities valued by Slytherin House, the House of the Serpent. We must *choose* to be in Gryffindor; like Harry we must choose to become members of the House of the Lion.

Chosing to do the right thing may not lead us to earthly rewards, as Cedric Diggory discoverd in *Harry Potter and the Goblet of Fire*. Cedric was a brave, honorable boy who valued fair play and who, unfortunately, crossed the path of Lord Voldemort at the wrong moment and ended up being murdered because of it. Dumbledore advised his students to remember Cedric Diggory "if the time should come when you have to make a choice between what is right and what is easy." (GF 724) Many have noted the similarities between the names of Cedric Diggory and the name of the character of Digory Kirke in C. S. Lewis's *The Chronicles of Narnia*. Digory Kirke, whose last name means "church," was the name of the brave boy in *The Magician's Nephew* who later became the old professor who befriended the Pevensie children in *The Lion, the Witch, and the Wardrobe*. Lewis thought of Digory as his alter-ego of sorts, and it is possible that Rowling was making a tribute to Lewis when she named one of her Triwizard Champions after him. Digory, when choosing to do the will of Aslan rather than his own will, was like Harry. Both had to make a choice between what is right and what is easy.

The idea that mankind must discern the nature of good and evil and choose between them is a theme in *The Lord of the Rings* as well. During the evil times faced by the heroes of that novel, Eomer asked, "How shall a man judge what to do in such times?" Tolkien's answer reveals a belief in moral absolutes:

> "As he ever has judged," said Aragorn. "Good and ill have not changed since yesteryear; nor are they one thing among Elves and Dwarves and another among Men. It is a man's part to discern them, as much as in the Golden wood as in his own house." (LOTR 428)

The denial of moral absolutes and the existence of "good" and "evil" is a philosophy of Lord Voldemort that Professor Quirrell has embraced:

"…A foolish young man I was then, full of ridiculous ideas about good and evil. Lord Voldemort showed me how wrong I was. There is no good and evil, there is only power and those too weak to seek it…" (SS 291)

"Why suffer a horrific death when you can join me and live?"—Quirrell/Voldemort to Harry in the film *Harry Potter and the Sorcerer's Stone* (2001)

Harry's response to this philosophy and the temptations that accompany it was to call Quirrell/Voldemort exactly what he is: "LIAR!" Harry shouted. (SS 294) Harry, like Rowling herself, believes that good and evil are very real, and chosing to do one or the other is a choice that we all must make, a choice that has eternal consequences.

An aspect of the power of choice that is emphasized in the final two Harry Potter novels is how a person's willful choice to do evil will damage that person's soul. Both in Christianity and in Harry's world, it is the choices that one makes in this life that will affect the fate of one's immortal soul in the next life.

2. Life after Death and the Immortality of the Soul

The Christian is taught not to fear death, because as it says in John 3:16, "For God so loved the world that he gave his only Son, so that everyone who believes in him may not perish but may have eternal life." (NRSV) Dumbledore teaches Harry throughout the series that he should not be afraid of death, because there are far worse things than dying. He encourages Harry to embrace death when it comes, for it is "like going to bed after a very, *very* long day. After all, to the well-organized mind, death is but the next great adventure." (SS 297)

Harry had to come to terms with his fear of the unknown when Sirius Black died in *Harry Potter and the Order of the Phoenix*. In the Department of Mysteries Harry encountered the veil that separates the world of the living and the dead. Upon a raised stone dais stood

> A stone archway that looked so ancient, cracked, and crumbling that Harry was amazed the thing was still standing. Unsupported by any surrounding wall, the archway was hung with a tattered black curtain or veil which, despite the complete stillness of the cold surrounding air, was fluttering very slightly as though it had just been touched. (OP 773)

The veil in the Department of Mysteries that separates the world from the living from the world of the dead is similar to the veil of the Temple in Jerusalem that separated the High Priest from God's presence in the Holy of Holies (2 Chronicles 3:14). Once a year, on the Day of Atonement, the High Priest could enter the Holy of Holies and be in the presence of God in order to offer the ritual sacrifice of animals' blood to make atonement for the sins of the people of Israel. The High Priest had to undergo a ritual purification before passing through the veil, for nothing unclean could enter the presence of God. (See Leviticus chapter 16.)

The symbolism of the "veil of death" can be found in Isaiah 25:7, where it is described as a shroud or sheet cast upon the entire human race:

> And he will destroy on this mountain the shroud that is cast over all peoples, the sheet that is spread over all nations; he will swallow up death forever. (NRSV)

Isaiah's prophecy of the destruction of the veil of death was fulfilled when Jesus Christ died on the cross. The blood that Jesus shed on the cross was the blood sacrifice that was necessary to make atonement for all of the sins of the world.

> Then Jesus cried again with a loud voice and breathed his last. At that moment the curtain of the temple was torn in two, from top to bottom. The earth shook, and the rocks were split. The tombs also were opened, and many of the bodies of the saints who had fallen asleep were raised. (Matthew 27: 50-52, NRSV)

In this passage is the image of the *torn* veil is quite similar to the "tattered black curtain" described by Rowling in *Harry Potter and the Order of the Phoenix.*

Hebrews chapter 10 explains that we now have access to God gained through Jesus "by the new and living way that opened for us through the curtain (that is through his flesh)." (Hebrews 10:20, NRSV) The blood sacrifice of Christ is what allows us to pass through the veil of death to be in the presence of God. It is the "gateway" (like Rowling's ancient archway) for the sheepfold. (John 10:9)

When Harry first encountered the veil, he was spellbound by the faint whispering, murmuring noises that only he and Luna Lovegood could hear. Later, after Sirius went beyond the veil, Harry grappled with the questions that have perplexed humankind since the beginning of our existence: *What happens when you die? Where do you go?*

When Harry talked with Luna about the death of her mother, Luna made an amazing claim:

"...it's not as though I'll never see Mum again, is it?"

"Er—isn't it?" said Harry uncertainly.

She shook her head in disbelief. "Oh, come on. You heard them, just behind the veil, didn't you?"

"You mean--"

"In that room with the archway. They were just lurking out of sight, that's all. You heard them." (OP 863)

After this conversation with Luna, Harry had the feeling that he would see his godfather Sirius again someday. Christians cling to the same hope of seeing loved ones who have "gone on," because of their faith in Jesus. Christ's death on the cross was a sacrifice for the sins of the world. This sacrifice is the ultimate act of love; it has the power to liberate humanity from the punishment that is due for our transgressions, the punishment given to our race in Eden. The punishment given by God for the sins of Adam and Eve was *death*.

3. The Power of Love and Self-Sacrifice

In the first four novels, Voldemort was unable to touch Harry because of the protection of Lily Potter's loving self-sacrifice:

"Your mother died to save you. If there is one thing Voldemort cannot understand, it is love. He didn't realize that love as powerful as your mother's for you leaves its own mark. Not a scar, no visible sign...to have been loved so deeply, even though the person who loved us is gone, will give us some protection forever." (SS 299)

THE LORD OF THE HALLOWS

Dumbledore again mentioned that Lily's blood shed in self-sacrifice was a powerful protection against evil in *Harry Potter and the Order of the Phoenix*, "Your mother's sacrifice made the bond of blood the strongest shield I could give you." (OP 836) Harry lost this protection in *Harry Potter and the Goblet of Fire* when Voldemort used Harry's own blood to return in the flesh. This event would contribute to Lord Voldemort's downfall in the seventh novel. There is a passage in *Goblet of Fire* that indicates that Dumbledore knew this would happen:

> "He said my blood would make him stronger than if he'd used someone else's," Harry told Dumbledore. "He said the protection my—my mother left me—he'd have it too. And he was right--he could touch me without hurting himself, he touched my face."
>
> For a fleeting instant, Harry thought he saw a gleam of something like triumph in Dumbledore's eyes. (GF 696)

Voldemort was able to possess Harry in Book 5 due to the fact that Lily's blood no longer offered Harry protection. However, this terrible circumstance led Harry to make an important discovery: the power that Lily had is a power that Harry has as well. It is the same power that is behind the enigmatic Locked Door in the Department of Mysteries:

> "It contains a force that is at once more wonderful and more terrible than death, than human intelligence, than the forces of nature...It is the power held within that room that you possess in such quantities and which Voldemort has not at all." (OP 843)

CHRISTIAN THEMES IN THE STORY OF HARRY POTTER

When Harry was possessed by Voldemort in *Order of the Phoenix*, he was able to save himself using the Power the Dark Lord Knows Not, the power of love.

Harry's friends have this power as well. Ron and Hermione risked their lives to help Harry to defeat evil many times throughout the series. The theme of self-sacrificial love is present from the first book onward, not just in the tale Lily's dying to save baby Harry from Voldemort, but in Ron's heroic actions in the giant chess game.

> "We're nearly there," he muttered suddenly. "Let me think—let me think…"
>
> The white queen turned her blank face toward him.
>
> "Yes…" said Ron softly, "it's the only way…I've got to be taken."
>
> "NO!" Harry and Hermione shouted.
>
> "That's chess!" snapped Ron. "You've got to make some sacrifices!" (SS 283)

Ron willingly sacrificed himself in the chess game to save his friends. By risking his life Ron allowed Harry to win the game, and then prevent Quirrell from obtaining the Philosopher's Stone.

Harry, like Frodo in *The Lord of the Rings*, tried to travel alone on his mission to destroy a great evil, but in both situations, their friends would not allow it. Both Rowling and Tolkien made a point about the importance of fellowship. The hero may save the world, but it is his friends who save him. Three hobbits from the Shire accompany Frodo on his mission, Sam, Merry, and Pippin:

> "Merry and I are coming with you. Sam is an excellent fellow, and would jump down a dragon's throat to save you,

if he did not trip over his own feet; but you will need more than one companion in your dangerous adventure." –Pippin (LOTR 102)

"You cannot trust us to let you face trouble alone...We are your friends, Frodo." –Merry (LOTR 103)

Frodo warned Sam of the dangers they would face, but Samwise was not deterred:

"But I am going to Mordor."
"I know that well enough, Mr. Frodo. Of course you are, and I'm coming with you."—Frodo and Sam (LOTR 397)

The love of his friends, especially that of Sam, is what sustains Frodo in his struggle to resist the influence of the Ring as he makes his arduous journey to Mordor and Mount Doom. Sam's devotion to Frodo is a selfless model of Christian love:

"It is going to be very dangerous, Sam. It is already danger-ous. Most likely neither of us will come back."
"If you don't come back, sir, then I shan't, that's certain," said Sam. *Don't you leave him!* They said. *I never mean to.* (LOTR 85)

Just as Frodo desired to complete his terrible journey alone, so did Harry insist upon going after the Philosopher's Stone by himself.

"I'll use the invisibility cloak," said Harry. "It's just lucky I got it back."
"But will it cover all three of us?" said Ron.
"All—all three of us?"

"Oh, come off it, you don't think we'd let you go alone?"
"Of course not," said Hermione briskly. "How do you think
you'd get to the Stone without us? I'd better go and look through
my books, there might be something useful…" (SS 271)

When the trio is faced with the task of getting past the giant
three-headed dog, Fluffy, all three of them realize the dangers that
await them.

"If you want to go back, I won't blame you," [Harry] said.
"You can take the cloak, I won't need it now."
"Don't be stupid," said Ron.
"We're coming," said Hermione. (SS 271)

In the adventure that followed, Ron bravely sacrificed himself to
save Harry and Hermione in the giant chess game. And then, after
solving the potions riddle, Hermione made a statement about what
personal qualities she values most: "Books! And cleverness! There
are more important things—friendship and bravery." (SS 287)

Dumbledore remembered Ron and Hermione as well as Harry
when he made his will. His intention was to have all three of them
go on the mission to destroy the Horcruxes together, knowing that
Harry should not face such terrible dangers alone. As Gandalf said,
with regards to Merry and Pippin going on the quest, "I think,
Elrond, that in this matter it would be well to trust rather to their
friendship than to great wisdom." (LOTR 269, emphasis mine).
Gandalf, like Dumbledore, knows that the love and loyalty of
friends is a powerful weapon against the darkness that threatens to
engulf the world. Love isn't just the power that allows Frodo and
Harry to save others, it is also the power that saves them from the
evil they must confront.

Rowling, in my opinion, has made a reference to Sam's loyalty and devotion at the conclusion of *Harry Potter and the Half-Blood Prince* when Ron and Hermione insist on going with Harry on his mission to destroy the Horcruxes. Sam Gamgee, in one of his most memorable speeches, reminds us that he and Frodo are characters in a story. Their adventure is one of the stories that stays in our hearts, long after the telling of the tale is done.

> "But that's not the way of it with the tales that really mattered, or the ones that stay in the mind. Folk seem to have been just landed in them usually—their paths were laid that way, as you put it. But I expect they had lots of chances, like us, of turning back, only they didn't." (LOTR 696)

Perhaps Rowling views Harry's story as one of the "tales that really mattered" when she wrote the ending of the sixth of Harry's adventures. At the close of the final chapter of *Harry Potter and the Half-Blood Prince*, Ron and Hermione express a devotion to Harry in words that echo Sam's selfless loyalty.

> "We'll be there, Harry," said Ron.
>
> "What?"
>
> "At your aunt and uncle's house," said Ron. "And then we'll go with you wherever you're going."
>
> "No," said Harry quickly; he had not counted on this, he had meant them to understand that he was undertaking this most dangerous journey alone.
>
> "You said to us once before," said Hermione quietly, "that there was time to turn back if we wanted to. We've had time, haven't we?"
>
> "We're with you whatever happens," said Ron.

4

Harry Potter and
The Bestiary of Christ

In addition to the themes of free will, good versus evil, life after death, the immortality of the soul, and the power of love, friendship, and self-sacrifice, the *Harry Potter* novels are rich in symbolism derived from ancient and Medieval folklore and legends. A wealth of information on Christian symbolism relevant to *Harry Potter* can be found in *The Bestiary of Christ* by Louis Charbonneau-Lassay. This book was published in French in 1940 and in English in the early 1990's. Much of the information in this book is a compilation of various Medieval bestiaries, which were treatises on animals and what they symbolized. Bestiaries were highly imaginative popular literature in Medieval times and were used to teach moral lessons and Christian theology. Some of the animal symbols in this book which are used in the *Harry Potter* novels include the lion, the serpent, the unicorn, the stag, the phoenix, the basilisk, and the weasel, among others. Our examination of animals used as symbols in the novels will begin with a closer look at the mascots of the four Hogwarts houses: the Slytherin serpent, the Gryffindor lion, the Ravenclaw eagle, and the Hufflepuff badger.

1. The Symbolism of the Four Houses

During Harry's first year at Hogwarts he is introduced to the Sorting Hat ceremony, a yearly ritual at the school in which the new students are sorted into one of four different houses. Each house was named after one of the four founders of Hogwarts: Salazar Slytherin, Godric Gryffindor, Rowena Ravenclaw, and Helga Hufflepuff. The hat sings a song to explain the qualities that the four founders of Hogwarts were seeking when selecting students for his or her house:

> *You might belong in Gryffindor*
> *Where dwell the brave at heart,*
> *Their daring, nerve, and chivalry*
> *Set Gryffindors apart;*
> *You might belong in Hufflepuff,*
> *Where they are just and loyal,*
> *Those patient Hufflepuffs are true*
> *And unafraid of toil;*
> *Or yet in wise old Ravenclaw,*
> *If you've a ready mind,*
> *Where those of wit and learning,*
> *Will always find their kind;*
> *Or perhaps in Slytherin*
> *You'll make your real friends,*
> *Those cunning folk use any means*
> *To achieve their ends. (SS 118)*

The conflict of good versus evil at Hogwarts focuses on the enmity between two houses that are always in direct opposition to each other: Gryffindor and Slytherin. Harry Potter, our heroic Gryffindor, is a model of what this house stands for: chivalry and courage. Draco Malfoy, Harry's Slytherin arch-rival, is also a model of his house's ideals: ambition and pure-blood supremacy. Even the two characters names reveal their allegiances. Likewise, Professor Albus Dumbledore, a Gryffindor, and Lord Voldemort, the Heir of Slytherin, have names that were carefully chosen for their symbolic meaning.

Harry's name could be thought of as the verb "to harry." The term "to be harried" means to be harassed or distressed by repeated attacks," as when Harry is harried by the many attempts Voldemort has made to kill him. The name *Potter* has symbolic meaning derived from the Bible, where God is referred to as a "potter," as in Isaiah 64:8: "But now, O Lord, thou art our father; we are the clay, and thou our potter; and we are all the work of thy hand." (KJV) Other references to God as the "potter" can be found in Jeremiah 18:5-6 and Romans 9:20-21.

The name Albus Dumbledore also has symbolic meaning. The name "Albus" means "white," and an alb is the white garment worn by a Catholic priest. *Dumbledor* is an archaic word that means bumblebee. Tolkien made use of the word *dumbledor* in The *Adventures of Tom Bombadil* which contains "Errantry," a poem which tells of a diminutive hero who vanquished the giant insects in battle. (*Tolkien Reader* 214) According to the *Bestiary of Christ*, the bumblebee was a symbol of the soul's survival after death. The bee disappears in winter and reappears in the spring, thus becoming a signifier of the Resurrection.

Draco Malfoy, on the other hand, has a name that has very negative connotations. Draco is the Latin word for "dragon" or "serpent," both traditional Biblical symbols of Satan, most notably the serpent who tempted Eve in the book of Genesis and the serpent described in Revelation 20:2, "...the dragon, that ancient serpent, who is the Devil and Satan..." (KJV) The surname *Malfoy* can be thought of as the French *mal foi*, which translates as "bad faith," so Draco Malfoy's name literally means "Dragon of Bad Faith" or "Serpent of Bad Faith."

The most extensive serpent imagery associated with any one character in the novels is that imagery which surrounds the supreme villain, Lord Voldemort. He is a descendant of Salazar Slytherin, the founder of Slytherin House. He, like his ancestor, is a parselmouth who can speak to snakes. Voldemort has a hairless, snake-like appearance, having two slit-like nostrils instead of a human nose. His loyal minions, the Death Eaters, are each identified by the Dark Mark, a distinctive snake and skull tattoo. This is a symbol from Christian art: the skull and serpent are often depicted at the foot of the Cross of Calvary. The skull represents death, the punishment for the sin of Adam, and it is symbolic of the fallen nature of mankind. According to Jewish legend, Adam's burial place was at Golgotha, the "place of the skull." The skull at the foot of the cross was there to represent Adam's skull, and the serpent was present as an allusion to Satan, the great tempter in the Garden of Eden who brought about the fall of mankind.

As the teenager Tom Riddle, Voldemort opened the Chamber of Secrets and unleashed the great serpent, the *basilisk*, upon the Hogwarts School. The basilisk, or cockatrice, is another symbol of Satan which is mentioned in Isaiah 14:29 (KJV): "Out of the serpent's root shall come forth a cockatrice and his fruit shall be a fiery flying serpent." In *The Bestiary of Christ*, the basilisk is described as a symbol of Satanic evil. This is mentioned in a description of a little country church that was decorated with "the image of a knight on foot striking a helmeted basilisk with his sword. It is the struggle between Good and Evil, so often and variously depicted, and could be seen as Christ fighting with Satan." (*Bestiary* 423) This imagery is found in *Harry Potter and the Chamber of Secrets* in the chapter that describes how Harry used the Sword of Godric Gryffindor to slay the basilisk.

The name *Godric* means "power of God," reminding us that the Christian, like Harry, will not be abandoned in his or her fight with the Great Serpent. We have the "power of God" on our side in our conflict with the Dragon. Also note that the surname *Gryffindor* can be thought of as the French *griffin d'or* which means "griffin of gold." The griffin, according to the bestiaries, is a symbol of Christ because of its dual nature: it is both lion and eagle, just as Christ is both God and Man. The eagle is a creature of the heavens, symbolizing the divine nature of Christ, and the lion is a creature of the earth, representing Christ the Man. The griffin's mastery of the earth and sky came to be associated with Christ's Ascension. The griffin was, through its association with Jesus Christ, thought to be the enemy of serpents and basilisks who, as previously mentioned, are symbolic of the Devil.

The eagle, mascot of Ravenclaw House, was a symbol of Baptism because the ancients believed the eagle's life was renewed by plunging itself three times into a body of water, hence its depiction on Christian baptismal fonts. The eagle was often depicted as a slayer of serpents in many cultures, and thus viewed as an enemy of Satan. Its ability to soar to great heights was associated with Christ's Ascension, as well as with St. John, the evangelist who was considered to be the most "intellectual" of the four gospel authors. This association of the high-flying eagle with great intellectual acumen may be the reason J.K. Rowling made it the mascot for Ravenclaw, whose motto is "Wit beond measure is man's greatest treasure." The eagles in Tolkien's *The Hobbit* and *The Lord of the Rings* have a brief but important role, used symbolically to represent Divine Providence or Divine Intervention.

That the Gryffindor mascot is a lion is not surprising; the lion is a Biblical symbol of Christ and a symbol of the Resurrection. In Revelation 5:5 Jesus is referred to as "the lion of the Tribe of Judah." The lion was also a symbol of the Resurrection to the early and medieval Christians because it was believed that lion's cubs were born dead. When the cubs were three days old, the father lion breathed on them and brought them to life, just as Christ lay in the tomb for three days before the Resurrection. This same symbolism of Christ the Lion is used by C. S. Lewis in *The Chronicles of Narnia*. The character of Aslan is a magnificent lion and a literary "Christ figure" who sacrifices himself to save the life of a human traitor. He is gloriously resurrected due to the workings of "Deeper Magic from Before the Dawn of Time." We know that Jo Rowling read and loved this story as a child, and I believe that Lewis's Narnian Chronicles had an influence on the plot and symbolism of the entire *Harry Potter* series.

J.K. Rowling's description of the Hufflepuff dormitories will seem familiar to fans of *The Hobbit* and *The Lord of the Rings:* There are "little underground tunnels leading to the dormitories, all of which have perfectly round doors, like barrel tops," she said in the Bloomsbury live online chat on July 30, 2007. This description sounds remarkably like the description Tolkien gave of Bilbo Baggins' home, a comfortable hobbit hole called Bag End. Bilbo's home is a cozy, luxurious tunnel-like construction with perfectly round doors.

Hufflepuff House is known for the virtues of loyalty and hard work, and is represented by a badger mascot. Perhaps a Narnian influence can be detected here as well: in Lewis' *Prince Caspian* the badger Trufflehunter is one of the Old Narnians that aids Caspian in the war with the wicked usurper, King Miraz. Trufflehunter the

Badger is loyal to Aslan even in the darkest of times. Trufflehunter's faith in the Great Lion remains strong, even when many other Narnians have ceased to believe. Lewis's character Drinian even uses the expression "loyal as a badger" in chapter two of *The Voyage of the* Dawn Treader. Likewise, there are many Hufflepuff students who are loyal to Harry: some are members of Dumbledore's Army, and many more are among the large number of Hufflepuff students who stand alongside the Gryffindors and Ravenclaws who fight to defend the castle in the Battle of Hogwarts.

2. The Slaying of the Unicorn

In addition to the lion and the griffin, another symbol of Christ is the unicorn. Ancient and Medieval lore indicates that a unicorn's horn possessed miraculous powers of healing. Anyone who drank from the horn would be protected from disease or poison. The *Dictionary of Symbolism* gives an account of the unicorn's power to cleanse water that has been fouled by a serpent:

> The early Christian *Physiologus* describes as follows the power of the horn to counter the effects of poison: before the other animals come to drink, "the snake comes forward and spits its venom into the water. The animals, however, knowing that the water is poisoned, do not dare to drink. They await the unicorn. The unicorn comes, goes right to the lake and makes a cross with its horn. This removes the effect of the poison. Only after the unicorn has drunk do the other animals approach and do likewise." (Biedermann 361)

Unicorns, which were once thought to be real animals, appeared in older translations of the Bible, such as the King James Version:

> "…his horns are like the horns of unicorns: with them he
> shall push the people together to the ends of the earth…"
> (Deuteronomy 33:17, KJV)
> "Will the unicorn be willing to serve thee, or abide by thy crib?
> Canst thou bind the unicorn with his band in the furrow? Or
> will he harrow the valleys after thee?" (Job 39:9-10, KJV)

These references to unicorns in the King James Bible occurred due to an error in translation. About three centuries before Christ, a group of scholars known as The Seventy translated the Old Testament from Hebrew into Greek. This translation is known as the Septuagint. The word for a type of wild ox, *re'em,* was translated *monokeros,* which means "single horned creature." The translators were unfamiliar with the word *re'em* because by that time the animal had become extinct. St. Jerome, in the late 4th century, used the Septuagint as the basis for his Latin translation of the Bible that was in use for many centuries. He translated the Greek *monokeros* as the Latin word *unicornis.* Many people understood this word to refer to the mythological unicorn, and therefore believed the animal must be real because it appeared in the Bible. Indeed, Rowling may know this story of why unicorns appeared in the King James Bible because it is apparent that she is familiar with the term *re'em.* She made use of this Hebrew word to refer to a rare golden ox whose blood gives the drinker immense strength. This reference can be found on page 36 of Rowling's own *Fantastic Beasts and Where to Find Them.* Perhaps she discovered the term when researching the lore of unicorns.

In addition to the creature's appearance in the Bible, the early Church fathers wrote about the unicorn as a symbol of Christ. According to St. Basil the Great (329-375 A.D.), "Christ is the power of God, therefore he is called the unicorn because the one horn symbolizes one common power with the Father." St. Ambrose

(339-397 A.D.) also saw the unicorn as a symbol of Christ: "Who is the unicorn but the only begotten Son of God?"

Because of these associations with Christ, both the lion and the unicorn appeared as Christ symbols in Medieval and Renaissance artwork. Reproductions of *The Lady and the Unicorn*, a set of famous tapestries from the Museum of Cluny in Paris, appear as wall hangings in the Gryffindor Common Room in all of the Warner Brothers Harry Potter films to date. A lion and a unicorn are depicted in each tapestry along with a female figure.

Another set of famous unicorn tapestries, currently housed in the Cloisters, the Medieval exhibit of the New York Metropolitan Museum of Art, is a set entitled *The Hunt of the Unicorn as an Allegory of the Passion*. These tapestries, woven in 1495-1505 in the Netherlands, depict the betrayal and passion of Jesus Christ as a unicorn hunt. Although the unicorn is killed in the sixth of the seven tapestries, he appears alive and well in the seventh tapestry. Here, the unicorn is a collared beast in a small enclosure, surrounded by a field of colorful flowers. "The Unicorn in Captivity" is symbolic of the resurrected Christ. A unicorn tapestry copied from this famous work of art appears in the film *Harry Potter and the Half-Blood Prince* (2009), and can be seen clearly behind Ginny Weasley when she takes Harry by the hand in front of the Room of

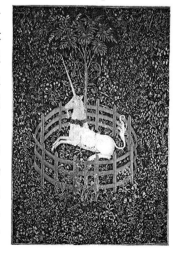

THE LORD OF THE HALLOWS

Requirement. In the second tapestry of this series, entitled "The Unicorn is Found," the unicorn dips his horn into a stream. Here, the unicorn is surrounded by other animals which are also Christian symbols; among them are the lion, the weasel, and the stag. All of these animal symbols are pertinent to this discussion of *Harry Potter.*

In the book, *The Unicorn Tapestries,* by Adolfo Salvatore Cavallo, the author explains the symbolism of the unicorn:

> Early bestiaries indicate that the unicorn dips its horn into water that wild creatures need for drinking in order to purify it of the poisons that serpents have spewed into it. The allegory is clear: Christ takes on the sins of Man and so purifies him in order to bring about his redemption. The serpent is the devil; the poison he introduces into the world (the water) is sin. (Cavallo 57)

In *Harry Potter and the Sorcerer's Stone,* Harry hears running water as he walks through the Forbidden Forest. He concludes that there must be a stream somewhere close by, and notices spots of unicorn blood along the path. (SS 251) He is aware that there is a creature in the forest that has been killing the unicorns. The stream and the slain unicorn both suggest the imagery of the medieval bestiaries as well as the iconography of *The Hunt of the Unicorn as an Allegory of the Passion.* Rowling's description of what Harry sees that night in the forest could be a scene from the crucifixion story that the tapestries portray:

Something bright white was gleaming on the ground. They inched closer.

It was the unicorn all right, and it was dead. Harry had never seen anything so beautiful and sad. Its long slender legs were stuck out at odd angles where it had fallen and its mane was spread pearly-white on the dark leaves.

Harry had taken one step toward it when a slithering sound made him freeze where he stood. (SS 255-256)

This is the hour of the Crucifixion, the hour of the Serpent's triumph. It was Voldemort who made the slithering sound over the dead leaves; he was the Great Serpent who murdered the unicorn. Harry's pain at encountering Voldemort in the forest is so great that he falls to his knees. (SS 256) The Dark Lord has done the unthinkable: he has been drinking the blood of the slain unicorn to sustain himself. His fear of death is such that he would slay the most worthy of creatures to sustain his unnatural life.

"…it is a monstrous thing, to slay a unicorn," said Firenze. "Only one who has nothing to lose, and everything to gain would commit such a crime. The blood of a unicorn will keep you alive, even if you are an inch from death, but at a terrible price. You have slain something pure and defenseless to save yourself, and you will have but a half-life, a cursed life, from the moment the blood touches your lips." (SS 258)

This passage echoes St. Paul's teaching on receiving Holy Communion, and those who receive it unworthily:

> Wherefore whosoever shall eat this bread, and drink this cup of the Lord, unworthily, shall be guilty of the body and blood of the Lord. But let a man examine himself, and so let him eat of that bread, and drink of that cup. For he that eateth and drinketh unworthily, eateth and drinketh damnation to himself, not discerning the Lord's body. (1 Corinthians 11:27-29, KJV)

According to St. Paul, to drink the blood of Christ unworthily at Communion is to drink damnation upon oneself. This parallels Fierenze's claim that Voldemort has done the very same thing by drinking the blood of a unicorn, thus drinking a terrible curse upon himself.

Harry had a very strange dream in *Harry Potter and the Prisoner of Azkaban*, which may provide a link between the unicorn and the next Christ symbol that we will examine.

> He was walking through a forest, his Firebolt over his shoulder, following something silvery-white. It was winding its way through the trees ahead, and he could only catch glimpses of it between the leaves. Anxious to catch up with it, he sped up, but as he moved faster, so did his quarry. Harry broke into a run, and ahead he heard hooves gathering speed. Now he was running flat out, and ahead he could hear galloping. (PA 265)

Was it a unicorn that Harry followed in his mysterious dream? Or was it something else? When Harry saw his corporeal patronus for the first time, he thought that, "It was as bright as a unicorn." (PA 385) But later, Harry will discover that the silvery-white creature that saved him from the Dementors wasn't a unicorn at all...

3. The Hunting of the White Stag

A Christ symbol that is closely related to the unicorn is the stag, whose earliest representation in Christian art can be found in the Roman catacombs and in baptismal font designs and basilica altar mosaics of subsequent periods. It appeared as a Christ symbol in bestiaries, in the stories of the lives of the saints, and in medieval romances, such as the *Queste del Saint Graal,* where the stag served as a guide toward the object of the quest, the Holy Grail.

The stag appeared as a symbol of Christ in the story of St. Eustace. This saint, like C. S. Lewis's fictional character Eustace Scrubb in *The Voyage of the* Dawn Treader, experienced a miraculous conversion. The pagan Eustace (Eustachius) was a Roman general who enjoyed hunting. On one hunting trip, Eustace tracked a stag through the woods and prepared to kill the magnificent creature. Just as Eustace was ready to slay the majestic stag, a miraculous vision appeared to the hunter: a vision of Christ crucified appeared between the stag's antlers. The hunter was converted to Christianity on the spot. To commemorate this miracle, the church of St. Eustachio in Rome was dedicated to him.

A similar tale of a hunter who converted due to a miraculous vision is in the story of St. Hubert. While out hunting on Good Friday the future saint encountered a stag with a crucifix between its antlers. A voice spoke to him from where the stag was. It asked why Hubert was pursuing him, and Hubert realized he had been searching for Christ for many years, and had finally found him. Hubert was converted at that moment. St. Hubert's desire to find Christ was a thirst for God that manifests symbolically as a stag. This symbol of the soul's thirst for God is derived from Psalm 42:1 (NRSV), "As a deer longs for flowing streams, so my soul longs for you, O God."

Because of the stag's longing for streams of water described in the Book of Psalms, it became associated with the soul's desire for purification through Baptism.

> Just as the deer devours the snake,
> Then rushes off his thirst to slake,
> Lets spring the venom wash away,
> So all is well, can Christian say,
> For he is saved, sin's trace is lost,
> When in baptismal font he's washed. (Biedermann 93)

This explains why the relief-work on many old baptismal fonts often includes representations of deer. Mosaics in some European

churches, such as the mosaic above the altar in Rome's Basilica of Saint Clement, sometimes depict a doe or stag drinking the water of life from the running stream described in Psalm 42. Early Christian texts such as *Physiologus* describe the deer as spitting water into every crevice in which poisonous snakes hide, then trampling on them, just as Christ strikes at the Devil with the heavenly water of Baptism. (Biedermann 92) The stag was thus seen as the symbol of the triumphant Christ. When a stag's antlers break, they regenerate, and for this reason the stag became a symbol of the Resurrection as well.

Other ancient lore associated the stag with the discovery of *dittany*, a miraculous herb that cures all wounds. In *Harry Potter and the Deathly Hallows*, Hermione carries a bottle of the essence of dittany to cure the wounds of her injured companions during their quest to destroy the Horcruxes. This miraculous liquid is mentioned first in Chapter 14 when Hermione heals the bleeding Ron Weasley, who has splinched himself while apparating. Hermione also uses dittany to heal Harry when he has been bitten by the snake Nagini in Chapter 17. In Cavallo's *The Unicorn Tapestries*, the author quotes from Margaret L. Freeman's book of the same title in the appendix, where it says, "Stags can shake off any arrows which they have received if they partake of the herb called dittany." (Cavallo 119) J. K. Rowling must have had some knowledge of this ancient lore of dittany because she made great use of it in *Deathly Hallows*.

In the Medieval religious story, *The Quest for the Holy Grail*, the Knights Galahad, Percival, and Bors were riding through the forest when they encountered a white hart escorted by four lions. The three knights followed the white hart, and it lead them to a chapel where the Mass was being sung. Inside the little church the four lions transformed into the four living creatures that symbolize the four evangelists (Matthew, Mark, Luke, and John), and the stag transformed into a man enthroned, Jesus Christ. The priest explained the symbolism of the miracle that the knights had witnessed. It is only after they have had the vision of the transformation of the white stag that they are able to find the Holy Grail. (Matarasso 243-245)

In *The Grail: Quest for the Eternal*, John Matthews explains the symbolism of the white stag with relationship to the Holy Grail quest:

> To reach the temple of the Grail, the knights who set out from Camelot must undergo many tests and experience terrible ordeals. But often, when the way seems darkest, the enigmatic white stag or hermit figure appears, to lead them forward through the mazes of forest and hill. In medieval iconography the stag was identified with Christ and the soul's thirst for God, which accounts for its appearance in this context. (Matthews 88)

THE LORD OF THE HALLOWS

In C. S. Lewis's *The Lion, the Witch, and the Wardrobe*, the author made use of the same symbolism that is found in the Grail legends. When Peter, Susan, Edmund, and Lucy Pevensie followed the white stag they were able to re-enter the wardrobe to return home. By following the white stag, the four protagonists were really following the Great Lion: that is to say, they were being obedient to Aslan's will. This parallels the story of the knights who follow the white stag to find Christ and the Grail.

The stag appears in Harry Potter's world as a symbol of his father. "Prongs" was the nickname given to Harry's father James, an animagus who could transform himself into a stag. In the third novel Rowling spoke to her readership through Dumbledore, who told Harry (and us) that the ones who love us never truly leave us, not even in death. When Harry suffered from attacks from soul-sucking Dementors in *The Prisoner of Azkaban*, he had to learn how to conjure a patronus to protect himself. The words *"Expecto Patronum!"* translate as "I expect a protector!" and protection arrived in the form of a luminous, graceful four-hoofed animal, which Harry initially mistakes for a unicorn. (PA 385) It is a luminous *stag*, the form his father once took when he was alive, and the brilliant patronus, like a guardian angel providing protection, drove away the darkness and despair of the Dementors. Harry's protector is a stag, which like the unicorn, is a symbol of Christ.

The stag's female counterpart is the doe. Just as the Knights of the Grail and heroes of Narnia followed the white stag, our hero must follow the silver doe in *Harry Potter and the Deathly Hallows*. "The Silver Doe" is one of the most beautiful chapters in the novel:

> A bright silver light appeared right ahead of him, moving through the trees. Whatever the source, it was moving soundlessly. The light seemed simply to drift toward him.
>
> He jumped to his feet, his voice frozen in his throat, and raised Hermione's wand. He screwed up his eyes as the light became blinding, the trees in front of it pitch-black in silhouette, and still the thing came closer…
>
> And then the source of the light stepped out from behind an oak. It was a silver doe, moon-bright and dazzling, picking her way over the ground, still silent, and leaving no hoofprints in the fine powdering of snow. She stepped toward him, her beautiful head with its wide, long-lashed eyes held high. (DH 365-366)

Just as King Arthur's knights followed the White Stag to find the Holy Grail, Harry followed the Silver Doe into the dark forest. The luminous creature led Harry to a frozen pool where, beneath the ice, lies a shape like "A great silver *cross*." (DH 367, emphasis mine) The Silver Doe had lead Harry to the Sword of Godric Gryffindor, which lay trapped beneath the frozen water. The apparent baptismal imagery in this scene will be discussed in Chapter Nine.

4. Phoenix Rising

The mythology of classical antiquity described the phoenix as a majestic bird which flew to foreign lands to gather fragrant herbs and spices to heap upon an altar, set fire to them, and then burn itself to ashes, only to rise from the pyre after three days time. The early Fathers of the Church logically saw this myth as a typological symbol of the death of Christ, who rose from the tomb on the third day.

THE LORD OF THE HALLOWS

The phoenix was adapted by the early Christians as a symbol of the Resurrection as early as the first century A.D. Drawings of the creature appear amongst the Christian murals and "graffiti" that identify the tombs of the martyrs in the catacombs beneath the city of Rome. St.Clement of Rome, who was pope at the end of the first century, wrote of the legend of the phoenix in his First Letter to the Corinthians. He used the story of how the bird died and rose again as a new phoenix to explain the Resurrection of the Christian faithful which will occur at the end of time:

> "Let us consider the strange sign which takes place in eastern lands, that is, in the regions near Arabia. There is a bird called the phoenix. It is the only one of its kind, and it lives for five hundred years. When the time for its dissolution in death approaches, it makes for itself a sepulcher of frankincense and myrrh and the other aromatics, into which, when the time is fulfilled, it enters and dies. From its decaying flesh a worm is born, which is nourished by the juices of the dead bird until it grows wings. Then, when it is strong, it takes up that sepulcher in which are the bones of the bird of former times, and carries them far from the land of Arabia to the city of Heliopolis in Egypt; and there, in the daytime, in the sight of all, it flies to the altar of the sun where it places them; and then it starts back to its former home. The priests then inspect the records of the times and find that it has come at the completion of the five hundredth year. Do we, then, consider it a great and wonderful thing that the Creator of the universe will bring about the resurrection of those who have served Him in holiness and in the confidence of good faith, when He demonstrates the greatness of His promise even through a bird?"—from the

HARRY POTTER AND THE BESTIARY OF CHRIST

First Letter to the Corinthians by St. Clement of Rome, 80 A. D. (Jurgens 8-9)

The Medieval bestiaries compared the phoenix, with the power to lay down his life and take it up again, to Jesus Christ. Like the lion, griffin, unicorn, and stag, the phoenix is a Christ symbol.

Pagans saw the phoenix as a symbol of the immortality of the human soul. In Mesopotamian and Egyptian art, this was symbolized by a winged solar disk, a depiction of the sun with wings. It is possible that this image had some influence on the Old Testament prophet Malachi who wrote: "...the Sun of Righteousness shall arise with healing in his wings." (Malachi 4:2, KJV) The *Sun* of Righteousness or *Sun* of Justice referred to by Malachi was later thought by the early Christians to be the *Son* of Righteousness or the *Son* of Justice who *rises*, that is, Jesus Christ the Resurrected Son. The image of the sun with wings was a symbol of the immortality of the soul, a symbol of resurrection which was also portrayed by the phoenix. We have seen the symbol of the winged solar disk portrayed as a physical object in Harry Potter's world: it is the Golden Snitch.

In *Harry Potter and the Deathly Hallows*, in the chapter entitled "The Will of Albus Dumbledore," the professor leaves Harry the first snitch he ever caught in a Quidditch match. The snitch is marked with the words, *"I open at the close."* When Harry goes to face his death at the climax of the novel, he opens the Golden Snitch to find the Deathly Hallow known as the Resurrection Stone hidden inside of it. Thus, Rowling has presented the readers with one resurrection symbol (the stone) hidden inside of another (the winged solar disk).

Harry is most fond of his holly and phoenix feather wand, which he chose over the all-powerful Elder Wand at the end of book seven. It contains one tail feather from Dumbledore's pet phoenix, Fawkes, as its power source. The wand is made of holly, and like its phoenix-feather core, the wood is symbolic also. Holly is said to be one of the plants used to make the Crown of Thorns. Another legend claims that it was used as the wood of the Cross of Calvary. Holly was thought to provide protection from lightning and to ward off evil spirits. Its evergreen leaves symbolize eternal life. Christian legends claim that holly berries were originally white but they were stained red by the Blood of Christ after he was crowned with thorns. Holly was also associated with Christmas because of a tale describing how the holly tree grew leaves out of season in order to hide Jesus, Mary, and Joseph from King Herod's soldiers. For this reason, it is miraculously evergreen. In the Cloisters of the Metropolitan Museum, in the unicorn tapestry entitled "The Unicorn is Killed and Brought to the Castle," a holly tree grows behind the creature's head, reminding the viewer that the unicorn is a symbol of Christ. In fact, holly appears in all but the first and last of the Cloisters' unicorn tapestries and in all six of the unicorn tapestries in the Cluny Museum's collection. The holly and phoenix feather wand was an important clue about Harry's destiny that has been present from the first book onward.

The symbolism of the phoenix has been important throughout the series. Harry met Fawkes, Dumbledore's pet phoenix, in the second book, *Harry Potter and the Chamber of Secrets*. Fawkes saved Harry's life by crying healing tears to heal a mortal wound Harry received from the deadly basilisk. The tears of a phoenix are the only known cure for the basilisk's poisonous venom. Fawkes's song gave Harry renewed strength and courage in *Harry Potter and the Goblet of Fire* when the young hero had to face Voldemort in the flesh during the wizard's duel in the churchyard. Dumbledore's patronus is a phoenix, and the name of the Anti-Voldemort league that Dumbledore established is called "The Order of the Phoenix." All of the good adult wizards that Harry admires—Dumbledore, McGonagall, Hagrid, Sirius Black, Remus Lupin, Tonks, Mad-Eye Moody, Kingsley Shacklebolt, and Mr. and Mrs. Weasley—are members of the new Order of the Phoenix. Harry's deceased parents, James and Lily, along with Ron's deceased uncles, Gideon and Fabian Prewett, and Neville's parents, Frank and Alice Longbottom, were all members of the original Order of the Phoenix during the First Voldemort War. We even witness Fawkes the Phoenix saving Dumbledore's life when Voldemort tries to use Avada Kedavra, the Death Curse, to defeat him: "Fawkes swooped down in front of Dumbledore, opened his beak wide, and swallowed the jet of green light whole." (OP 815) Only the phoenix, like Christ, could take the curse of death upon himself and rise again in glory, unharmed. From the earliest days of Christianity, the phoenix was a symbol of the believer's hope of Resurrection at the end of the world. Its ascension into the heavens, like that of the eagle, symbolized the soul's desire for union with God. At the funeral which concludes the sixth book, Harry saw smoke rising from the white flames around Dumbledore's body, and "Harry thought, for one heart-stopping moment, that he saw a phoenix fly joyfully into the blue." (HBP 645)

5. Weasley is Our King!

In *The Hunt of the Unicorn as an Allegory of the Passion,* the tapestry entitled "The Unicorn is Found," depicts the unicorn dipping its horn into a stream to purify it. The unicorn, a Christ figure, is surrounded by other animals, some of which are Christ symbols as well, such as the lion and the stag. But standing near the stream closest to the unicorn's horn is a small, slender creature which may represent a genet, an ermine, or a weasel. The much-maligned weasel is a favorite animal of author J. K. Rowling. Generally speaking, calling someone a "weasel" is usually an insult. Indeed, there are numerous examples of Draco Malfoy calling Harry's best friend Ron Weasley such insulting names as "the weasel" or "the weasel king." In *Harry Potter and the Order of the Phoenix*, the Slytherins mock Ron Weasley with badges that proclaim "Weasley is Our King!" sarcastically and sing a song by the same title which has lyrics that insult Ron's Quidditch-playing skills and make fun of his family's poverty.

The Bestiary of Christ reveals a totally different perception of weasels. "Although the weasel is the smallest of carnivores, it can win combats with much bigger animals than itself," thus "the weasel is the perfect symbol of a Christian who, no matter how weak in himself, can still triumph over Satan, the most terrifying monster of hell." (*Bestiary* 147) This passage calls to memory the scene in *Harry Potter and the Deathly Hallows* in which Ron must confront his deepest fears and insecurities when he is tempted by the locket of Slytherin Horcrux, which contained a fragment of the Dark Lord's soul. Voldemort spoke to Ron in this scene as a deceiver and a tempter, just as the Father of Lies, Satan, deceives and tempts the Christain to sin. But like the Christian who is weak in himself and yet with God's help can triumph over Satan, Ron, with Harry's encouragement, rejected Voldemort's lies and used the Sword of Godric Gryffindor to destroy the locket Horcrux.

The Bestiary of Christ also describes the weasel as the "symbol of the perfect disciple;" Ron is Harry's devoted follower, sidekick, and best friend. The weasel is also described as a "symbol of paternal affection," reminding the reader of Molly and Arthur's great love for their children. Weasels are said to be the enemies of *rats* (Peter Pettigrew) and *snakes* (Slytherin bullies, Death Eaters, and

Lord Voldemort himself). The *Bestiary* also describes the weasel as "the most implacable vanquisher of that terrifying reptile, the *basilisk…*" (*Bestiary* 148-149). According to this legend, the weasel must sacrifice its own life to slay the basilisk. In *Harry Potter and the Chamber of Secrets,* Ginny Weasley almost loses her life in the basilisk's lair. She is saved only when Harry slays the basilisk with the Sword of Gryffindor and uses one of the creature's fangs to destroy the diary Horcrux, thus freeing Ginny from Tom Riddle's enchantment.

Another bit of weasel lore known to J. K. Rowling is that "Weasels are careful to feed on *rue* before fighting with snakes…" (*Bestiary* 150) In *Harry Potter and the Half-Blood Prince,* the poison that Draco Malfoy intended for Dumbledore was mistakenly consumed by Ron Weasley (an example of a *weasel* being poisoned by a *serpent*). During Ron's recovery in the hospital wing, Madame Pomfrey gives Ron essence of rue as an antidote to the poison.

The *Bestiary* also mentions a type of weasel called the *ermine,* whose brown coat turns white in the winter. The ermine, due to its white color, symbolizes purity, especially feminine virtue. The ermine's white coat disappears into the snow in the winter months and re-appears in the spring when its fur turns brown again. For this reason the ermine was a symbol of death and resurrection. Please make note of the presence of the letters e-r-m-i-n-e in Hermione's name. What do you think of when Ron mumbles her name in his sleep as "Er-my-nee"? Er-mi-ne?

Otters are also part of the weasel family, so it's no surprise that the Weasleys live near the village of Ottery-St.Catchpole, and that Hermione, the eventual wife of Ronald Weasley, has an otter patronus. In Christian art, the otter is sometimes used as a symbol of Christ's righteousness. (Apostolos-Cappadonna 263).

In The Unicorn Tapestries the weasel appears alongside its

peers: it is as courageous as the lion, as pure as the unicorn, as nurturing as the deer, and like its fellows, it is the sworn enemy of the serpent. Ron and his family have been well named indeed.

Clearly, Rowling has a thorough knowledge of ancient and medieval Christian symbolism, and has made extensive use of this iconography throughout the entire *Harry Potter* series. In the next chapter we will examine the desire for physical longevity and the effects of sin on the immortal human soul in the light of Christian theology and the philosophy of J. R. R. Tolkien.

5

The Lord of the Horcruxes

J. K. Rowling invented the word *Horcrux* to describe a magical object used to contain a portion of a human soul. The making of such a soul container is achieved through murder and the most forbidden dark magic. Although the word *Horcrux* and its specifics are unique to Rowling's fiction, the concept of attaining immortality in the flesh by locking one's heart or soul away in a physical object is a very ancient one. An examination of the writings of J. R. R. Tolkien will clarify our understanding of what both Rowling and Tolkien have to say about this concept.

In Tolkien's fiction, it is apparent that no created being is completely evil in the beginning. Frodo speaks for Tolkien when he says:

> The Shadow that bred them can only mock, it cannot make: not real new things of its own. I don't think it gave life to the orcs: it only ruined them and twisted them. (LOTR 893)

Tolkien believed that not even the Dark Lord Sauron was wicked in the beginning:

> Sauron was of course not "evil" in origin. He was a spirit corrupted by the Prime Dark Lord (the Prime sub-creative Rebel) Morgoth. He was given an opportunity of repentance, when Morgoth was overcome, but could not face the humiliation of recantation, and suing for pardon. (*Letters* 190)

In Appendix A of *The Return of the King*, Tolkien explained Sauron's "return" after his body had been destroyed:

> …the bodily form in which he long had walked perished; but he fled back to Middle-earth, a spirit of hatred borne upon a dark wind. He was unable ever again to assume a form that seemed fair to men, but became black and hideous… (LOTR 1013)

Voldemort also existed as a malicious evil spirit after the loss of his body, described as "mere shadow and vapor." (SS 293) When he regained a physical form in *Harry Potter and the Goblet of Fire* his visage is described from Harry's point of view as both frightening and repulsive:

> But then, through the mist in front of him, he saw, with an icy surge of terror, the dark outline of a man, tall and skeletally thin, rising slowly from inside the cauldron. […]
> The thin man stepped out of the cauldron, staring at Harry…and Harry stared back into the face that had haunted his nightmares for three years. Whiter than a skull, with

wide, livid scarlet eyes and a nose that was flat as a snake's
with slits for nostrils...

Lord Voldemort had risen again. (GF 643)

Voldemort was horrible in appearance, possessing a body with
only a fragmented and corrupt soul. The Dark Lord Voldemort,
by prolonging his existence through the making of Horcruxes,
had done something quite similar to what the Dark Lord of
Middle-earth had done.

Sauron, as chief representative of Evil in Middle-earth's Third
Age, prolonged his influence long after his body had been destroyed
by containing his "essence," his *soul* if you will, in the One Ring of
Power. Tolkien explained the folly of creating such an object:

> The Ring of Sauron is only one of the various mythical
> treatments of the placing of one's life, or power, in some
> external object, which is thus exposed to capture or destruc-
> tion with disastrous results to oneself. (*Letters* 279)

Rowling's Dark Lord Voldemort, has done exactly what Tolkien
described by splitting his soul into pieces to create his Horcruxes.
In his "flight from death," Voldemort sought to become immortal
in the physical realm, but this is at best an extended longevity, not
true immortality. In September 1954 Tolkien wrote, "...that Men
are essentially *mortal* and must not try to become *immortal in the
flesh*." (*Letters* 189, emphasis mine) In another letter Tolkien wrote
in 1958, he explained that this desire for longevity is how Sauron
tempted lesser beings to follow him, which led to their demise:

> To attempt by device or "magic" to recover longevity is thus
> a supreme folly and wickedness of "mortals." Longevity or

counterfeit "immortality"…is the chief bait of Sauron—it leads the small to Gollum, and the great to a Ringwraith. (*Letters* 286)

Sauron and Voldemort have much in common: neither was wholly evil in the beginning. Both had opportunities to show remorse or repent of their evil acts, but both refused. Each made himself vulnerable by placing his life essence or soul in an external object or objects with disastrous results. Let's examine the origins of Lord Voldemort and keep Sauron's folly in mind.

In *Harry Potter and the Chamber of Secrets*, Harry learned that "Tom Marvolo Riddle" is an anagram of "I am Lord Voldemort." Tom Riddle, detesting his muggle father's name, chose a new name for himself, a name befitting a Dark Lord whose flight from death led him to commit acts of supreme evil. But like Sauron, Voldemort was not always evil. His birth name, Tom Riddle, gives us a clue to his origins.

The name "Tom" in Hebrew means "innocence" or "wholeness, perfection, purity." (Sidi 89) This is the state of a soul that is holy, that is, a soul that is whole and complete. The young boy who later became Voldemort revealed his true nature in his first meeting with Dumbledore: "You dislike the name 'Tom'?" (HBP 274) It is obvious to Professor Dumbledore that the response to that question is an affirmative answer. The boy's surname, Riddle, also gives us a clue. One definition of the word *riddle* is "to perforate with holes." Tom's soul has indeed been perforated, riddled, even *torn* by his willful acts of evil: Tom Riddle abandoned his innocence and damaged his immortal soul in the making of Horcruxes. Professor Slughorn gave us a definition of the term Horcrux as "the word used for an object in which a person has concealed part of their soul." (HBP 497)

THE LORD OF THE HORCRUXES

As Tolkien explained in his letters, the notion of concealing one's soul in an object in order to gain physical immortality is a motif found in mythology, folk lore, and fairy tales. One such tale is the Russian fairy tale that inspired Igor Stravinsky's famous ballet, *The Firebird*. In the tale, the hero, Prince Ivan, rescues a beautiful princess from captivity by the evil wizard, the Immortal Kashchei. The evil sorcerer Kashchei gained his physical longevity by concealing his heart (that is, his soul) inside of a magical egg. With the aid of the benevolent Firebird, Prince Ivan is able to destroy the egg, defeat the now mortal Kashchei, and rescue his true love, the princess. At the tale's conclusion, the knights of the realm who had been turned to stone (petrified) by the evil wizard were restored to life again as a result of the heroic actions of Prince Ivan and the Firebird. Clearly this Russian fairy tale has many parallels with the plot of *Harry Potter and the Chamber of Secrets*: the young hero, Harry, rescues his true love, Ginny, from an evil wizard, Tom Riddle, who has concealed part of his soul in an object, the diary. With the aid of a benevolent firebird, Fawkes the Phoenix, Harry defeats the basilisk, destroys the diary, and rescues Ginny. At the end of the novel, the Hogwarts students who had been petrified are returned to life again.

Tolkien was very familiar with this type of fairy tale, a story in which a character prolongs the span of human life by removing his heart (a metaphor for the human soul), and hiding it away in an object. Tolkien described this in his essay "On Fairy Stories."

> ...the life or strength of a man may reside in some other place or thing; or in some part of the body (especially the heart) that can be detached and hidden in a bag, or under a stone, or in an egg. (*The Tolkien Reader* 44)

The notion that the heart can be hidden away to prolong one's life is alluded to in *Harry Potter and the Deathly Hallows* when Ron and Harry examine the locket Horcrux.

> "Can you feel it, though?" Ron asked in a hushed voice, as he held it tight in his clenched fist.
> "What d'you mean?"
> Ron passed the Horcrux to Harry. After a moment or two, Harry thought he knew what Ron meant. Was it his own blood pulsing through his veins that he could feel, or was it something beating inside the locket, like a tiny metal heart? (DH 276)
> From time to time Harry thought, or perhaps imagined, that he could feel the tiny heartbeat ticking irregularly alongside his own. (DH 278)

Rowling also made use of this fairy tale concept in "The Warlock's Hairy Heart" from *The Tales of Beedle the Bard*. The villain of that tale, like the Immortal Kashchei and Lord Voldemort, locked his heart away inside an object to gain invulnerability. Dumbledore's commentary on this tale says that, "The resemblance of this action to the creation of a Horcrux has been noted by many writers." (TBB 58) One can only wonder if Dumbledore (or J. K. Rowling) has been reading Tolkien. Perhaps this is Rowling's way of telling us that her readers should. I believe it is significant that the passages from *Harry Potter and the Deathly Hallows* quoted above are from the chapter called "The Thief" in which Harry, through Voldemort's eyes, sees Gregorovitch the wandmaker tortured for information about a *thief*. Remember what Tolkien said about the dangers of placing one's heart or soul in an external object: it is "exposed to capture or destruction with disastrous results to oneself." (*Letters* 279) The object may be stolen or destroyed: both Tolkien and

THE LORD OF THE HORCRUXES

Rowling emphasize this in their fiction. Gollum (as Smeagol) stole Sauron's ring from his cousin Deagol, Bilbo Baggins took the ring from Gollum, and eventually gave it to Frodo who embarked on a quest to destroy it in the fires of Mount Doom. Dumbledore was able to obtain the ring Horcrux from Marvolo Gaunt's home and destroy it. Regulus Black was able to steal the locket Horcrux from the cave of the Inferi. Harry, Ron, and Hermione were able to break into Bellatrix Lestrange's Gringott's vault to steal the cup Horcrux. And finally, the trio was able to gain access to the Room of Hidden Things to search for the diadem Horcrux, which was destroyed in the fire conjured by Vincent Crabbe. J. K. Rowling said that the two Bible quotations found in the graveyard scene in Godric's Hollow "sum up—they almost epitomize the whole series." (Adler 2) With reference to the Horcruxes, let's examine the Bible quotation on the Dumbledore family tomb:

> Where your treasure is, there will your heart be also. (DH 325)

This quotation is from Matthew's gospel, from Christ's Sermon on the Mount. To put the quote in context, this is what Christ had to say about earthly treasures:

> Do not store up for yourselves treasures on earth, where moth and rust consume and where thieves break in and steal; but store up for yourselves treasures in heaven, where neither moth nor rust consumes and where thieves do not break in and steal. For where your treasure is, there will your heart be also. (Matthew 6:19-21, NRSV)

There is a lesson in this that Dumbledore learned but Voldemort did not: do not put your heart and soul in the material wealth and pleasures of this world, because these treasures do not last and can be taken from you. They are temporal pleasures, finite like life itself. Rather, store up treasures in Heaven, which, like your soul, is eternal. Unfortunately, the sinful nature of human beings often prevents us from doing this.

When young Tom Riddle asked how a Horcrux is made, Slughorn explained that this is done by splitting one's soul and hiding part of it in an object outside of the body. Then, said Slughorn, "Even if one's body is attacked or destroyed, one cannot die, for part of the soul remains earthbound and undamaged." (HBP 497) When Riddle seeks the knowledge of how to split one's soul, Slughorn's response is chilling.

> You must understand that the soul is to remain intact and whole. Splitting it is an act of violation, it is against nature. [And it is done] by an act of evil—the supreme act of evil: By committing murder. Killing rips the soul apart. (HBP 497-498)

A Judeo-Christian explanation of the effects of evil (sin) upon the soul is essential to fully understanding this passage. A Biblical Hebrew lexicon reveals that the word *ra'a* means "to be evil," and one definition of this term translates as "to break, shatter; to be broken in pieces." To do evil, to sin against God, means literally *to ruin your soul by breaking it into pieces*. This is exactly what Voldemort has done by creating his Horcruxes. But once a soul is broken, can it be mended? Harry, Ron, and Hermione discussed this in Chapter Six of *Harry Potter and the Deathly Hallows*.

"Isn't there any way of putting yourself back together?" Ron asked.

"Yes," said Hermione with a hollow smile, "but it would be excruciatingly painful."

"Why? How do you do it?" asked Harry.

"Remorse," said Hermione. "You've got to really feel what you've done. There's a footnote. Apparently the pain of it can destroy you. I can't see Voldemort attempting it somehow, can you?" (DH 103)

Rowling has demonstrated in this passage that she has a clear understanding of how difficult repentance can be. To be truly repentant for one's sins is to be destroyed, to allow the old self to die in order to be born again in Christ. This is what the sinner must do in order to make his or her broken soul whole again. There are no temporal earthly pleasures or possessions worth more than the human person's immortal soul. Not only has Dumbledore learned this lesson, he also sees that Harry is living proof of the value of living free from the temptations of physical longevity and earthly treasures.

In spite of all the temptations you have endured, all the suffering, you remain pure of heart, just as pure as you were at the age of eleven, when you stared into a mirror that reflected your heart's desire, and it showed you only the way to thwart Lord Voldemort, and not immortality or riches. (HBP 511)

This passage refers back to Dumbledore's earlier quote in *Harry Potter and the Sorcerer's Stone*, in which he explained how humans usually choose "as much money and life as you can want," that is, they choose what's worst for them. This is a Biblical lesson:

> What shall it profit a man if he shall gain the whole world and lose his own soul? (Mark 8:36)

During the folly of his youth, Dumbledore learned of the fatal weaknesses of evil. Evil embraces power, pride, pleasure, materialism, self-centeredness, and hate. Evil cannot comprehend the value of weakness, humility, suffering, death, selflessness, and love. Once again Dumbledore shares his keen understanding of Voldemort's folly:

> I do not think he understands why, Harry, but then he was in such a hurry to mutilate his own soul, he never paused to understand the incomparable power of a soul that is untarnished and whole. (HBP 511)

Harry, Ron, and Hermione, as protagonists in this adventure, represent a trinity of such untarnished souls, not completely unlike the Grail knights Sir Galahad (the Pure), Sir Percival (the Fool), and Sir Bors (the Wise). In the next chapter we embark on a quest for the historical and literary predecessors of the Deathly Hallows. Let us pursue that flightly temptress, Adventure…

6

The Quest for the Hallows

Before we begin our quest for the Hallows, we must ask: what are hallows? The noun *hallow* means "a holy person or saint." "Hallows" is a word that refers to "the shrines or relics of saints." The verb "to hallow" means "to make holy, to sanctify, to purify" or "to honor as holy, to regard and treat with reverence or awe" as in the Lord's Prayer: "Our Father who art in Heaven, *hallowed* be thy name…" The October 31st celebration of Halloween is also known as All Hallows Eve, or the Eve of All Saints. All of this information combined with what was revealed in Book 6 about the Horcruxes seemed to indicate that the final volume of Harry, Ron, and Hermione's adventures would be a quest novel, not unlike the Christian myths of the quest for the Holy Grail. In some legends of this quest, King Arthur's knights are actually searching for four Grail Hallows:

1. the *Sword* of King David or, (alternately)
   the *Sword* that beheaded John Baptist
2. the *Dish* of the Last Supper

3. the Holy Grail *Cup*

4. the *Spear* of Longinus (also referred to as "the Spear of Destiny")

The cup, dish, and the spear are part of a larger collection of objects known as the *Arma Christi*, or Articles of the Crucifxion of Christ. There may be a correspondence between the lore of the four Grail Hallows and the four suits of the Tarot deck: swords, disks, cups, and wands. When the title of the final novel was released, I considered these correspondences, then looked for parallels in Harry's world. I expected the Sword of Gryffindor to play an important role in the final book, and it did. The dish or disk has a parallel in the Locket of Slytherin, and the cup is present as the Cup of Hufflepuff. But what of the spear? I examined the parallel with the four suits of the Tarot, and realized that a wand would be a suitable quest object in this story about wizards. I expected the Spear of Destiny would have a parallel as the *Wand of Destiny* in the wizarding world, and when the seventh novel was released, I discovered that this was indeed the case.

The legend of the Spear of Destiny developed from a passage in the Gospel of John, in which Jesus is found dead on the cross: "Instead, one of the soldiers pierced his side with a spear, and at once blood and water came out." (John 19:34, NRSV) Tradition derived from the non-canonical Gospel of Nicodemus gave this Roman soldier a name: Gaius Cassius Longinus. A sculpture of the legendary saint by the brilliant Italian artist Gian Lorenzo Bernini (1598-

1680) can be seen in Saint Peter's Basilica in Rome. Longinus is depicted holding the Holy Lance in his right hand. In 326 A.D. St. Helena, the mother of Constantine the Great, discovered relics thought to be the *Arma Christi* while on a pilgrimage in Jerusalem. Among the relics were the True Cross of Christ's crucifixion, the crown of thorns, the pillar at which Christ was scourged, and the Holy Lance. A legend later associated with this Holy Lance claimed that whoever possessed it would be able to conquer the world. A group of knights found a lance believed to be the Lance of Longinus beneath St. Peter's Cathedral in Antioch during the First Crusade. Possession of the alleged Holy Lance spurred the crusaders on to victory.

Harry Potter enthusiasts should notice that "Antioch Peverell" is the name of one of the three brothers who once possessed the Deathly Hallows. Antioch was the brother who wielded the Elder Wand, also known as the Wand of Destiny. Throughout history there have been many legends surrounding the relics that were thought to be the Lance of Longinus, the Holy Lance that came to be known as The Spear of Destiny. Likewise in the fictional wizard-

ing world of Harry Potter there were many legends surrounding the Elder Wand. Like the would-be conquerors throughout history who thought that the army who possessed the Spear of Destiny would be invincible, in Harry's world, the wizard who possessed the Elder Wand was thought to be unbeatable.

One candidate for the title of Holy Lance, allegedly the spear that was found by St. Helena and once belonged to Constantine the Great, was possessed by the Holy Roman Emperors. It was believed to have contained one of the nails used in the crucifixion. This lance was called the Hofburg Spear, and it was kept in Austria's Hofburg Museum until Adolf Hitler had it removed. On March 12, 1938 Hitler went to the Hofburg Museum to visit the supposed Holy Lance on the very same day that Nazi Germany took control of Austria. Hitler believed this relic was truly the Spear of Destiny, and possession of it would make him invincible. On October 13, 1938 Nazi troops moved the Hofburg Spear from Vienna to Nuremberg where it was on display at St. Katherine's Church for much of the Second World War. During the Allied Forces' bombing of Germany the spear was moved to a secure underground bunker in Nuremberg.

It is interesting to note that in Harry's world, the dark wizard Gellert Grindelwald, who was obsessed with the Wand of Destiny, was kept in a prison called Nurmengard.

The Hofburg Spear came into the hands of U. S. troops under the command of General Patton on April 30, 1945 at 3:00 p.m. when Nuremburg Castle was captured. Hitler committed suicide on April 30, 1945 at 3:30 p.m., just a half hour after he lost his "Spear of Destiny." The lance was returned to the Hofburg Museum in January 1946, where it has remained until this day.

Note that Hitler's defeat takes place in 1945, the same year that Dumbledore defeated the dark wizard Grindelwald and became the new owner of the Wand of Destiny. When asked if it was a coincidence that Grindelwald was defeated in 1945, Rowling said, "No. It amuses me to make allusions to things that were happening in the Muggle world…" (Anelli, 16 July 2005)

Hitler's obsession with the Spear of Destiny may have been the result of his passion for the operas of German composer Richard Wagner. Wagner's opera *Parsifal*, composed in 1882 was one of Hitler's favorites. The story of the opera is about Parsifal (known as Percival in the English versions of the tale), who is one of the knights who is questing for the Grail Hallows. The opera's plot is partially derived from *Parzival*, a German Medieval romance written in 1202-1210 by the poet Wolfram von Eschenbach. In the opera, the Spear of Destiny is glorified.

Wolfram's *Parzival* differs from Wagner's opera in many ways, most notably in the portrayal of the Grail itself. Wagner's Holy Grail is the traditional cup that one would expect, but in Wolfram's version of the tale, the Holy Grail is a *stone*. Why Wolfram chose to portray the Grail as a stone rather than as a cup was a mystery that perplexed scholars for many centuries. A recent piece of scholarship may have solved that mystery.

In the book *Gemstone of Paradise: The Holy Grail in Wolfram's Parzival*, author G. Ronald Murphy, a Jesuit priest, explains that the grail stone in Wolfram's romance was probably an altar stone, symbolic of the stone that was rolled across the entrance of Jesus's tomb before the resurrection. Father Murphy thought that Wolfram may have been inspired to imagine the Holy Grail as a stone because of his encounter with a portable altar of the type used on the crusades. This small altar was a container for holy relics (hallows), as well as holding the consecrated bread of the Eucharist inside it beneath the removable altar stone.

Father Murphy translated the Latin inscription on one such an altar as follows: "The altar of Christ's cross is one with this table, and this is therefore the proper place for the sacrifice of the victim who secures life." He later wrote, "This is the wood and the stone that guarantee the passage of Good Friday to Easter Sunday, death to life. The portable altar, and perhaps *this* very portable altar, is Wolfram's special stone of Resurrection, the phoenix stone in Wolfram's language..." (Murphy 185)

Indeed, this is how Wolfram describes the stone. In A. T. Hatto's English translation of *Parzival*, the passage describing the powers of the Grail Stone, or Stone of Resurrection, reads as follows: "By virtue of this Stone the Phoenix is burned to ashes, in which he is reborn—Thus does the Phoenix moult his feathers! Which done, it shines dazzling bright and lovely as before." (*Parzival* 239) According to Wolfram, the phoenix's power of Resurrection is from the power of the Grail Stone. In *Harry Potter*, Dumbledore hides the Deathly Hallow known as the Resurrection Stone within the Golden Snitch, a physical representation of the winged solar disk, a phoenix symbol. One symbol of resurrection is hidden inside of another.

Wolfram von Eschenbach was known to have an interest in alchemy. In alchemical language the Holy Grail, or phoenix stone, was in fact the Philosopher's Stone. The Medieval romance of the quest for the Holy Grail, like the alchemist's path to the creation of the Philosopher's Stone, is symbolic of the pursuit of spiritual perfection. That J. K. Rowling is aware of the connection between Wolfram's Grail Stone and the alchemical Philosopher's Stone is suggested in a footnote on page 99 of Rowling's *The Tales of Beedle the Bard*. Here, Rowling prompts her readers to make the connection between the Philosopher's Stone and the Resurrection Stone from "The Tale of the Three Brothers."

> Many critics believe that Beedle was inspired by the Philosopher's Stone, which makes the immortality-inducing Elixir of Life, when creating this stone that can raise the dead. (TBB 99)

I had developed my theory of *Parzival*'s Grail Stone as the inspiration for the Resurrection Stone Deathly Hallow in 2007, before

THE QUEST FOR THE HALLOWS

The Tales of Beedle the Bard was published. When reading Rowling's footnote from page 99 in December of 2008, I was delighted. I see this footnote as evidence that my theory of the hallows is a plausible one. Two of the three Deathly Hallows of Rowling's fiction—the Wand of Destiny and the Resurrection Stone—seem to have been inspired by the Grail Hallows of Arthurian legend. The legendary knight Parzival, or Perceval, was the hero of many Medieval romances, one of which was *La Folie Perceval*. Perceval in this version of the tale was thought to have been influenced by the character of Payne Peveril in *Fulke le Fitz Waryn* (1260 A.D.). A Welsh poem called *Peveril* also featured a character similar to Perceval. Perhaps the name "Peverell" (the surname of the three brothers who possessed the Deathly Hallows) may have been derived from *Peveril*. Antioch Peverell was the master of the Elder Wand, and Cadmus Peverell held the Resurrection Stone. But what of the third Deathly Hallow, the Invisibility Cloak of Harry's ancestor Ignotus Peverell? For the answer, perhaps we must turn to the ancient mythology of the British Isles.

The legend of the "Thirteen Treasures of Britain" also known as the "Thirteen Hallows of Britain" describes an impressive col-

lection of magical objects that would not seem out of place in Harry's world. The twelfth treasure, for instance, is a magical chessboard with "living" chess pieces, not unlike the Wizard's Chess game that Ron Weasley is so fond of playing. The thirteenth hallow in this collection is known as "The Mantle of Arthur" with the power to make the wearer invisible. This is very much like the Invisibility Cloak that was given to Harry by Dumbledore during his first Christmas at Hogwarts, the cloak that is the third of the Deathly Hallows.

THE LORD OF THE HALLOWS

Rather than four Grail Hallows or thirteen Hallows of Britain, Rowling creates a *trinity* of Deathly Hallows, represented by a vertical line and circle contained within a triangle. This is the symbol that was mistaken for the "Peverell coat of arms" by Marvolo Gaunt. (HBP 207) The vertical line represents the Elder Wand, or Wand of Destiny, which is *all-powerful*. The circle represents the stone with the power of *resurrection*, and finally, the triangle represents the cloak with the power to make the wearer *invisible*. Thus, the three Deathly Hallows are that which is *all-powerful*, the power of *resurrection*, and the presence that is *invisible*. In Christianity, this could symbolize the Holy Trinity: the *all-powerful* Father, the *resurrected* Son, and *invisible* presence of the Holy Spirit.

To possess the three Deathly Hallows is to become the Master of Death. But should any human being possess such god-like power?

Both Voldemort and the teen-aged Dumbledore sought immortality in the physical world. Both sought to be Masters of Death: Voldemort, by committing murders to create Horcruxes, and Dumbledore by trying to unite the three Deathly Hallows. Voldemort (whose name, you recall, means "flight from death") feared death above all else, and was willing to commit any crime to gain immortality in this world. Dumbledore, on the other hand, realized the error of his ways, and learned that death is not to be feared, but to be welcomed. In the end Dumbledore was not afraid to give up his life "for the greater good" and embark on his "next great adventure." Death as a theme in the writings of Tolkien and Rowling will be examined in the next chapter.

7

The Last Enemy

Frodo heard a sweet singing running in his mind: a song that seemed to come like a pale light behind a grey rain-curtain, and growing stronger to turn the veil all to glass and silver, until at last it was rolled back, and a far green country opened before him under a swift sunrise. (LOTR 132)

The passage quoted above describes one of Frodo's dreams, perhaps a dream of the Undying Lands far across the sea to the west of Middle-earth. In Peter Jackson's film adaptation of *The Return of the King*, Tolkien's evocative description of Frodo's glimpse behind the veil has been transformed into dialogue: during the siege of Minas Tirith, Gandalf and Pippin have a conversation about death in which the young hobbit learns that death is not the end of the soul's existence. Death is everywhere in *The Lord of the Rings*. It is present in the realm of the physical, that is, in the literal deaths of Boromir, Denethor, King Theoden, and countless others who fought in the War of the Ring. The theme is apparent in the realm of the supernatural: there are encounters with the spectral barrow-wights and with the restless spirits that haunt the Paths of the Dead. A setting for one near-death encounter for Frodo is provided by the eerie Dead Marshes. The hallows of Rath Dinen are the location of Lord Denethor's attempt to burn his son Faramir alive upon his own funeral pyre, followed by Denethor's own suicide. Tolkien uses the term "hallows" to refer to the burial chambers of the former kings and stewards of Gondor. In Jackson's film, *"Death!"* is the battle-cry of the Rohirrim as they ride to war against the terrible armies of Mordor.

Harry Potter is also surrounded by literal and symbolic death. Harry, the son of murdered parents, attends a school that is haunted by numerous ghosts. He duels Voldemort in a church graveyard after witnessing Cedric Diggory's death at the conclusion of the Triwizard Tournament. He can see the thestrals, skeleton-like horses that are only visible to those who have seen death. Harry is able to hear the voices whispering behind the veil that separates the living and the dead in the Department of Mysteries, and then witnesses the horror of his godfather Sirius Black falling through the veil, never to return to the world of the living. In a scene reminiscent of Frodo's trek through the Dead Marshes, Harry and Dumbledore enter the cave where the locket Horcrux was once hidden. They are attacked by the Inferi, animated corpses that try to drown intruders who dare to touch the water in which they hide.

Death personified as the "Grim Reaper" has a presence in both narratives. The skeletal figure of the Reaper, enshrouded in his black hooded cloak, seems to have inspired Tolkien's Nazgul (Ring Wraiths) and Rowling's Dementors. Frodo's encounter with the Ring Wraiths at Weathertop is similar to Harry's first terrifying meeting with a Dementor in *Harry Potter and the Prisoner of Azkaban*. When Frodo was attacked by the Wraiths, he heard "a

faint hiss as of venomous breath and felt a thin piercing chill."
(LOTR 190-191) Then later, "A breath of deadly cold pierced him
like a spear." (LOTR 208) When Harry met the Dementor on the
train, he heard a "long, slow, rattling breath" and "an intense cold
swept over them all." (PA 83) In a later encounter with the Nazgul,
one of the Black Riders flew overhead upon his winged Fell Beast,
and "Frodo felt a sudden chill running through him and clutching
at his heart; there was a deadly cold, like the memory of an old
wound, in his shoulder." (LOTR 378) When Harry tried to save
Sirius Black from the Dementors, he felt the "familiar, icy cold
penetrating his insides." (PA 383) Notice the similar ways in which
the wizards defend themselves (and others) from the dreadful creatures. When Gandalf repelled the Nazgul, it was with a "shaft of
white light" (LOTR 792) which was also described as "white fire."
(LOTR 802) Likewise the Dementors can only be driven away with
a patronus: Harry "thought he saw a silvery light growing brighter
and brighter…The blinding light was illuminating the grass around
him…" (PA 384-385) Rowling has explained in interviews that the
Dementors represent depression, and has spoken candidly about
her personal battles with that malady:

> "It was entirely conscious. And entirely from my own expe-
> rience. Depression is the most unpleasant thing I have ever
> experienced. It is that absence of being able to envisage that
> you will ever be cheerful again. The absence of hope. That
> very deadened feeling which is so very different from feel-
> ing sad. Sad hurts but it's a healthy feeling. It's a necessary
> thing to feel. Depression is very different."—J. K. Rowling,
> as quoted in the first edition of *The Magical Worlds of Harry
> Potter* (Colbert 57)

Similarly, Tolkien has described the Lord of the Nazgul as, "a spear of terror in the hand of Sauron, shadow of despair," (LOTR 800) and also named him the "Captain of Despair." (LOTR 801) Could the depression or despair referred to by both writers be caused by a fear of death or a fear of loved ones dying? Perhaps the Nazgul King gave us an answer when he said to Gandalf, "Old fool! This is my hour. Do you not know Death when you see it?" (LOTR 811)

In both narratives, the presence of death (and all of the symbolism associated with it) serves to reinforce the notion that death is a major theme both works. Let us examine three different Christian attitudes towards death. In the book *Catholic Christianity*, author Peter Kreeft explains that since death is *natural, unnatural,* and *supernatural,* Christians have three attitudes toward it:

> Since it is natural, we honestly confront it and accept it as a fact of our being, instead of avoiding it by endless diversions of our attention or, by living in denial, pretending it is not there. Since it is also unnatural, the inescapable punishment for sin, we hate it and fight it as our enemy, "the last enemy" (1 Cor. 15:26). Finally, since it is also supernatural, transformed by Christ's Resurrection, we welcome it. (Kreeft 135)

Harry encounters all three of these attitudes towards death in the septology. The first attitude, that death is natural and we must accept it, is something that Harry must confront at a very young age. Although Harry's parents were murdered during his infancy, he believed that they were killed in a car accident until he found out the truth at age eleven. He had to accept death as a part of life while growing up an orphan. The stages of grief that Harry experiences when learning to cope with the murders of Cedric Diggory and Sirius Black are part of his maturation process during adolescence, but like his parents' murder, these were "unnatural" deaths. Harry encounters the attitude that death is unnatural in the graveyard in Godric's Hollow when he reads the quotation from First Corinthians 15:26 on his parents' tombs. He doesn't know what the quote means in the context of Scripture, but assumes that it is an unnatural idea, a Death Eater idea. (DH 328) Hermione corrects him on this false assumption, introducing a supernatural interpretation of death in which we live beyond it. This supernatural interpretation is in accordance with Dumbledore's belief that death is the next great adventure. He believed that we shouldn't flee from Death but should greet it as an old friend as in "The Tale of the Three Brothers." (TBB 93)

J. K. Rowling has declared that death is a central theme of the books. In an interview from February 2008 she said, "I believe it was Tolkien who said that all the important books deal with death. And there's some truth in that because death is our destiny and we should face up to it." (*El Pais*, February 8, 2008) This quote seems to indicate that Rowling is familiar with Tolkien's views on death and its importance as a literary theme. She has not revealed if she merely heard about Tolkien's beliefs from someone else, or if she has read a quotation of this nature in one of his biographies or personal writings. In Tolkien's published works and letters, there isn't a quote that is an exact match for the one to which Rowling is referring, but in his published letters there are many quotations about death and immortality being the most important themes in his story of the Ring. In 1958 he wrote of *The Lord of the Rings*: "I might say that if the tale is 'about' anything it is not as seems widely supposed about 'power'....It is mainly concerned about Death and Immortality; and the 'escapes': serial longevity, and hoarding memory. " (*Letters* 284)

THE LORD OF THE HALLOWS

The escape from death that Tolkien mentioned, serial longevity, is present in Rowling's work in the form of the Nicholas Flamel's Philosopher's Stone, Voldemort's Horcruxes, and Dumbledore's desire to possess and unite the three Deathly Hallows. Of these methods of cheating death, the making of Horcruxes is the most wicked and the most similar to the evil of Sauron's Ring. The elves of Middle-earth are guilty of "hoarding memory" and being resistant to change. This fault is due to their great age, but is hardly evil. Perhaps Dumbledore's pensieve could be viewed as a device for memory hoarding. Snape's lifelong devotion to Lily is admirable because it is his love for her that facilitates his redemption, but his refusal to let go of the past could also be an example of the negative aspects of hoarding memory. He would not let go of his feelings of hatered and jealousy of James Potter, and this animosity was transferred to Harry without justification.

Tolkien identified *The Lord of the Rings* as a tale about "Death and the desire for deathlessness." (*Letters* 203) When he became aware of the dominance of this theme in his work he wrote, "But certainly Death is not an Enemy! The elves call 'death' the Gift of God (to Men)." (*Letters* 267) Tolkien took the supernatural attitude toward death: it is not an Enemy. Rowling allows Harry to experience three different attitudes toward death--the natural, unnatural, and supernatural--to have him gain, at the tender age of seventeen, the wisdom that other far older wizards have had a lifetime to learn.

As with life after death, although to a lesser degree, there does appear to be a "continued", subtle progression of a belief in God (or at least some kind of "higher power")

8

Belief in God in the World of Harry Potter

"How in the name of heaven did Harry survive?" asked Professor McGonagall at the beginning of *Harry Potter and the Sorcerer's Stone.* (SS 12) This is the first of many examples of how the language of Christianity is used throughout the series. In book one there is a reference to the concept of sin in the warning given to those who would steal from the Gringotts goblins: "Enter stranger, but take heed of what awaits the sin of greed." (SS 72) Harry, Ron, and Hermione even manage to escape from a deadly plant called the Devil's Snare. (SS 277-278) In *Harry Potter and the Chamber of Secrets,* Mr. Weasley asks, "Good lord, is it Harry Potter?" (CS 39) Draco refers to Harry as "Saint Potter, the Mudbloods' friend." (CS 223) Dumbledore even leads the Hogwarts students and faculty in "a few of his favorite carols" at Christmastime. (CS 212) In *Harry Potter and the Prisoner of Azkaban* the manager of Flourish and Blotts says "thank heavens" (PA 53), Draco Malfoy says "God" (PA 113), Hagrid utters "Gawd knows." (PA 274), and Remus Lupin says

Many characters, even purebloods who would not necessarily have much knowledge of "Muggle religion" do say things that would only be known about (e.g. Saints) if they knew about them (and believed in them)

"My God." (PA 363) Lupin also helps Harry learn the difference between losing one's life and losing one's soul. (PA 247) In these numerous references and in many others, there is evidence of a belief in the Christian God in the world of Harry Potter.

and tells him that losing ones soul is the worst case scenario

> "I like to play around with names, and I collect unusual ones from all sorts of sources, like maps, books of Saints."—J. K. Rowling on September 8, 1999

St. Mungo's Hospital for Magical Maladies and Injuries may have been named after both one of Rowling's fictional wizards and a real-world Christian saint. St. Kentigern, whose nickname was "St. Mungo," is the patron saint of Glasgow, Scotland. St. Mungo preached the gospel in Scotland in a manner similar to St. Patrick of Ireland, who converted a multitude of pagans to the Christian faith.

> "Hedwig was a saint, a Medieval saint."—J. K. Rowling on October 20, 2000

Harry's owl Hedwig bears the name of a Catholic saint as well. St. Hedwig was a Cistercian sister who had an order of nuns named after her. The Order of the Sisters of St. Hedwig has the chief aim of caring for and educating orphaned children. When Hedwig the owl dies tragically in Book 7, this may be read symbolically as the end of Harry's childhood. He is no longer the orphaned "Boy Who Lived," needing the protection given by adults. Harry has now become a man who must face his destiny as the "Chosen One."

"Honestly, Hermione, you think all teachers are saints or something," snapped Ron. (SS 183) Ironically, this quote was taken from a conversation about Severus Snape, the most enigmatic character in the whole series. The name *Severus* is an appropriate name for a character with potential for both great evil and even greater good, considering the name's associations in Christianity's long history. The Roman Emperor Lucius Septimus Severus was responsible for the massacre of 19,000 Christian men, women, and children during the persecutions of   202-211 A. D. The name Severus then would seem to be appropriate for the Death Eater Snape, who was permanently branded with the snake and skull tattoo of Voldemort's minions. But Severus Snape abandoned his service to the Dark Lord upon learning of the murder of his childhood friend and secret love, Lily Evans Potter. Severus pledged his loyalty to Dumbledore and became a member of the Order of the Phoenix, risking his life as a spy and as the secret protector of Lily's son, Harry. Severus Snape was murdered, poisoned by the snake Nagini under Voldemort's command. When Harry learned the truth about his former antagonist, he was able to forgive the man he loathed for seven years. In the Epilogue, we learn that Harry has named one of his sons after him. Harry tells young Albus Severus that Snape was "the bravest man I ever knew." Many readers of the Harry Potter series expected Snape to die a violent but heroic death in the final novel, and I count myself among those who predicted it. *The Catholic Encyclopedia of Saints* lists no less than twelve saints named Severus, many of whom were martyred for the love of Jesus Christ. Severus Snape, with a martyr's courage, risked his life and ultimately died for one he loved as well.

God is mentioned by the good wizards throughout all seven novels, and in the series there is even the hint of wizards serving in religious orders or as clergymen. For example, in *Harry Potter and the Order of the Phoenix*, it is revealed that only wizards can come back as ghosts (OP 860). An observant reader might recall that among the Hogwarts ghosts we have "The Fat Friar," the ghost

[handwritten marginal note:] to add however that this Monk chose to become a ghost rather than "join"

[handwritten marginal note:] So this man, who was a wizard, was also a Christian and apparently a Monk also. So he at least had a definitive faith

of Hufflepuff House. When Harry sees him for the first time, he is saying, "Forgive and forget." (SS 115) This ghost was apparently both a wizard and a clergyman in his lifetime. Also notice the group of ghostly, "gloomy nuns" that are present at Nearly Headless Nick's Deathday Party in *Harry Potter and the Chamber of Secrets*. (CS 132) In the corridors of Hogwarts there are paintings of sinister-looking monks (PA 101) as well as drunk monks (HBP 351). And at Christmastime Sir Cadogan's party included "a couple of monks, several previous headmasters of Hogwarts, and his fat pony." (PA 230)

In *Harry Potter and the Goblet of Fire*, the duel between Harry and Voldemort takes place in a churchyard. In the American edition of this novel there is a cross atop a tombstone clearly visible in Mary Grand Pre's illustration for Chapter 33. During the graveyard battle Harry

> ...dived behind a marble angel to avoid the jets of red light and saw the tip of its wing shatter as the spells hit it. Gripping his wand more tightly, he dashed out from behind the angel... (GF 668)

Even if this doesn't convince the reader that Divine Providence is involved, symbolically, at least, Harry has a "guardian angel." Even more intriguing is this passage from the fifth novel, when a golden statue of a wizard "flung out its arms, protecting Harry from the death curse." (OP 813) This action is symbolic of Christ on the cross, who spread his arms to protect humanity from the curse of death.

In *Harry Potter and the Deathly Hallows*, Rowling's use of Christian references and images becomes more obvious than in the previous novels. Good wizard characters say "thank God" (Harry on page

74, Molly on page 78, Ron on page 142), and there are jokes about a wizard being "saint-like" or "holy" (George on page 74). That George Weasley would call himself "holy" ("hole-y") refers to his missing ear, which was cursed off during a battle with the Death Eaters. St. George was a Christian saint, who, according to pious legends, was a dragon slayer. He took up arms against Satan who appeared to him in the form of a mighty serpent.

Harry witnesses a wizarding wedding performed by the same tufty-haired wizard who presided over Dumbledore's funeral. This wizard clergyman refers to Bill and Fleur as "two faithful souls" (DH 145). On page 154 Auntie Muriel says that Elphias Doge thought Dumbledore was a "saint." Ron says "God" again on page 165, and when Ted Tonks hears of a courageous attempt to retrieve the Sword of Gryffindor, he says "God bless 'em" with reference to Ginny, Neville, and Luna on page 298. One intriguing passage on page 284 describes Harry burying Alastor Moody's magical eye and identifying the spot by making a small *cross* on a nearby tree. There are references to heaven and hell in this novel also. When Voldemort offers Neville Longbottom a place among his Death Eaters, Neville responds, "I'll join you when hell freezes over!" (DH 731). A final reference can be found in the Epilogue when Ron tells his daughter, "Thank God you inherited your mother's brains." "Ron, for heaven's sake!" is Hermione's half-amused response to her husband's comment (DH 756).

9

The Downfall of Evil

By the end of chapter 15 of *Deathly Hallows,* Harry, Ron, and Hermione have been on their mission to destroy Horcruxes for over four months without making much progress. They have found only the locket but they have no means of destroying it. The evil presence of the soul fragment in the locket steadily increases their fears and anxieties. Harry is unable to conjure a patronus and has severe pain in his scar while wearing it. The locket makes Ron so irritable that he and Harry have the most explosive argument in the history of their friendship (DH 306-308), and Ron abandons the quest, leaving Harry deeply depressed and Hermione in tears (DH 310). The power that the locket has to bring out the worst in the three heroes is a power that tempts them towards evil thoughts. It is not unlike the evil power of Sauron's ring in J. R. R. Tolkien's *The Lord of the Rings.* The influence of the dark lord Sauron acting through the One Ring breaks apart the "fellowship" of the nine heroes who set out to destroy it. Likewise, the evil influence of the dark lord Voldemort acting through the locket places a rift between

Ron and his best friend Harry, and between Ron and the girl he loves, Hermione.

Early in the chapter called "Godric's Hollow," Harry's despair is overwhelming:

> They had discovered one Horcrux, but they had no means of destroying it: The others were as unattainable as they had ever been. Hopelessness threatened to engulf him. (DH 313)

But it is when Harry begins to lose hope in the chapter entitled "Godric's Hollow" that Rowling uses the strongest Christian imagery in the series thus far. Harry sees the "little church whose stained-glass windows were glowing jewel-bright" and hears the sound of Christmas carols which "grew louder as they approached the church. It made Harry's throat constrict, it reminded him so forcefully of Hogwarts." (DH 323-324)

Then, as Harry and Hermione walk through the churchyard, they discover the gravestones of Kendra and Ariana Dumbledore, and of James and Lily Potter. The fact that these tombs are found in a churchyard means that the wizard and witches buried there were laid to rest in *hallowed* ground, which means the Dumbledores and the Potters were given a Christian burial. That James and Lily may have belonged to a church or believed in the Christian religion isn't such a radical idea as some might think. In a 2004 interview at the Edinburgh Book Festival, J. K. Rowling was asked if Harry Potter has a godmother. Her response was:

> "No, he doesn't. I have thought this through. If Sirius had married…Sirius was too busy being a rebel to get married. When Harry was born, it was at the very height of Voldemort fever last time so his christening was a very hurried, quiet affair with just Sirius, just the best friend. At that point it looked as if the Potters would have to go into hid-

ing so obviously they could not do the big christening thing and invite lots of people. Sirius was the only [godparent], unfortunately."

In this interview, Rowling revealed that Harry was christened, meaning that he was baptized as an infant. Further proof that the Dumbledores and the Potters may have held Christian beliefs can be found in the quotations from the New Teastament which are inscribed on their grave markers.

> Harry stooped down and saw, upon the frozen, lichen-spot-ted granite, the words KENDRA DUMBLEDORE and, a short way below her dates of birth and death, AND HER DAUGHTER ARIANA. There was also a quotation: *Where your treasure is, there will your heart be also.* (DH 325)

This inscription is from the Gospel of Matthew, chapter 6, verse 21, which should be examined in the context in which it appears in the Bible: This quotation is from Christ's "Sermon on the Mount."

> Do not store up for yourselves treasures on earth, where moth and rust consume and where thieves break in and steal; but store up for yourselves treasures in heaven, where neither moth nor rust consumes and where thieves do not break in and steal. For where your treasure is, there will your heart be also. (Matthew 6:19-21, NRSV)

This passage warns against storing up earthly treasures, as Voldemort did by using valuable objects such as Slytherin's ring and locket, Hufflepuff's cup, and Ravenclaw's diadem to create Horcruxes in attempt to cheat death and gain physical immortality. In his youth, Dumbledore did something similar by seeking the earthly treasures known as the Deathly Hallows in order to become the master of death. Unlike Voldemort, Dumbledore learned that earthly treasures can be lost or stolen. He learned not to try to escape from death, but to embrace it. Dumbledore realized that the only immortality worth having is not in this life, but in the life one receives after death. In the graveyard scene, Harry has the notion that Albus Dumbledore may have chosen the inscription on Kendra and Ariana's tomb himself. What we know of his experiences seems to indicate that he did.

Later in this chapter, Harry reads the writing on his parents' grave markers, encountering the second Bible quote Rowling used in the novel:

> *The last enemy that shall be destroyed is death.*
> Harry read the words slowly, as though he would have only one chance to take in their meaning, and he read the last of them aloud. " 'The last enemy that shall be destroyed is death'..." A horrible thought came to him, and with it, a kind of panic. "Isn't that a Death Eater idea? Why is that there?"
> "It doesn't meaning defeating death in the way the Death Eaters mean it, Harry," said Hermione, her voice gentle. "It means...you know...living beyond death. Living after death." (DH 328)

Indeed, Hermione's interpretation is closer to the truth than Harry's. The Bible verse quoted here is from St. Paul's First Letter to the Corinthians, chapter 15, verse 26. Paul wrote to the Corinthians about Christ's resurrection being an indicator that Christ's followers would also be resurrected. In the Resurrection, death would truly be destroyed, and the faithful will "live beyond death" as Hermione described it.

Before they leave the churchyard, Hermione conjures a wreath of Christmas roses to lay upon the tomb of James and Lily. According to the tradition of Christian symbolism, the Christmas Rose is a symbol of the Nativity. The symbolism of the Holy Family of Joseph, Mary, and the infant Jesus can also be found in the monument of the Potter family, a memorial sculpture that depicts James, Lily, and the infant Harry.

This hauntingly beautiful chapter takes place on Christmas Eve. In the works of Lewis and Tolkien, the significance of Christmas cannot be overlooked. The four protagonists in *The Lion, the Witch, and the Wardrobe* receive gifts, weapons they will need to fight against the White Witch, from Father Christmas. They learn that Aslan is on the move and the White Witch's reign over Narnia is soon to end. The timeline that Tolkien devised for *The Lord of the Rings* shows that the nine heroes of *The Fellowship of the Ring* departed from Rivendell on December 25th. This was the beginning of their quest to destroy the One Ring , an event that would result in the downfall of the dark lord Sauron. According to Tolkien, Middle-earth's future is our past and present. Tolkien chose the December 25th date to foreshadow that in Middle-Earth's future, the Incarnation would occur that day, an event that marked the beginning of the end of mankind's enslavement to sin and the defeat of Satan.

The White Witch and Sauron are the "Satans" of the fictional universes they inhabit. If they knew that the events occurring at Christmastime would lead to their destruction, we could surmise that these adversaries would cry out in rage at their impending doom.

On page 342, Harry and Hermione, disguised as a middle aged couple, make a narrow escape from the trap set for them by Voldemort.

THE LORD OF THE HALLOWS

And then his scar burst open and he was Voldemort and he was running across the fetid bedroom, his long white hands clutching at the windowsill as he glimpsed the bald man and the little woman twist and vanish, and he screamed with rage, a scream that mingled with the girl's, that echoed across the dark gardens over the church bells ringing in Christmas Day...

Voldemort's wail of frustration, piercing the cold night air at just the very moment the church bells proclaimed the birth of Christ, reminds me of an English Christmas tradition.

An old Christmas Eve custom called ringing the Devil's Knell, persists in the town of Dewsbury in Yorkshire. The practice sprang up around the folk belief that the Devil dies each year at the moment when Christ is born. The Church bells still toll on Christmas Eve in Dewsbury announcing the Devil's demise. (Gulevich 183)

This tradition is also found in Ireland.

Many believed spirits walked abroad on Christmas Eve and deemed it wiser not to venture outdoors after dark. About an hour before midnight, church bells all over Ireland began to ring. This tolling, known as "the Devil's funeral" or the Devil's Knell, announced the death of the Devil, who was believed to expire annually on Christmas Eve with the birth of Jesus Christ. (Gulevich 286)

Harry had escaped from being murdered by Voldemort once again, not on the Eve of All Hallows, but on Christmas, the holiest night of the year. Rowling brilliantly sounded the Devil's Knell in triumphant counterpoint to the Dark Lord's scream of rage: this event heralds the beginning of Harry's triumph and serves as a warning to the Dark Lord that his days are numbered.

It is on the day after Christmas that Harry and his friends begin to make real progress in accomplishing their mission to defeat Voldemort. Just as King Arthur's knights followed the white stag through the forest to find the Grail Chapel, Harry followed the silver doe to a frozen forest pool where he saw a shape like "a great silver cross" (367). It was the Sword of Gryffindor hidden beneath the ice. The sword is one of the most fundamental Christian symbols:

> The Cross is God's sword, held at the hilt by the hand of Heaven and plunged into the world not to take our blood, but to give us His. (Kreeft 224)

Harry, while wearing the locket, tried to retrieve the sword, but the Horcrux around his neck began to choke him. It was when Harry began to drown that Ron returned to save his life. Proving himself to be a true Gryffindor, Ron pulled the sword from the water and severed the locket's hold on Harry. Voldemort, like Satan the Father of Lies, made a desperate effort to claim Ron as his own, and Ron, like the weasel who strikes against the venomous serpent, was able to strike the first fatal blow against Voldemort by destroying the locket Horcrux with Gryffindor's sword.

In terms of Christian symbolism, this chapter gives us two sacramental images, *baptism* (Ron, like John the Baptist, draws Harry up from the water) and *reconciliation* (Ron is truly sorry for abandoning Harry and is forgiven by him). Ron's destruction of the locket was the third Horcrux to be eliminated. Prior to this event, Harry had destroyed the Diary of Tom Riddle with a basilisk fang in *Chamber of Secrets*, and Dumbledore had destroyed Marvolo Gaunt's ring with the Sword of Gryffindor sometime before Harry's sixth year at school. During the Battle of Hogwarts Ron thought of a way to destroy the Cup of Hufflepuff, and Hermione accomplished the deed with the use of a basilisk fang. Following this event was the accidental destruction of the Diadem of Ravenclaw by Vincent Crabbe, who unleashed *fiendfyre*. This magical fire nearly killed Draco Malfoy, but Harry, showing mercy and compassion for his enemy, risked his life to save Draco from the flames. Draco's salvation was dependent on Harry, just as the sinner is dependent on Christ for salvation from the fires of Hell. After the diadem was destroyed only Nagini the snake and one other soul fragment remained. When these remaining links to eternal life have been severed, Voldemort will be mortal again.

10

Frodo and Harry as Christ Figures

In *Harry Potter and the Deathly Hallows*, Harry emerges as a "Christ figure." This is a literary term that indicates that a particular fictional character is Christ-like in some ways, but not an allegorical substitute for Jesus Christ. Harry is not the first fantasy hero to play this role in fiction. There is a literary precedent for this in the fantasy novels of J.R.R. Tolkien and C. S. Lewis.

In *The Lord of the Rings*, Frodo Baggins is a Christ figure. An early indication of Tolkien's intent to present him as such can be found in *The Fellowship of the Ring*. Following the Nazgul attack at the Ford of Bruinen, Frodo awakens after being unconscious for three days. This, of course, is a parallel to Christ's three days in the tomb. According to Peter Kreeft in *The Philosophy of Tolkien* there are Christ figures in *The Lord of the Rings* and everywhere in literature, and in life. "This should not surprise us," said Kreeft, because "Christ is the central point of the whole human story from the beginning in the Mind of its Author." (Kreeft 54) In addition to

identifying Frodo as a Christ figure on page 183, Kreeft also identifies Frodo as a Marian figure, claiming that Frodo's *fiat*, "I will take
the Ring though I do not know the way," (LOTR 264) is very similar to Mary's "Let it be done to me according to your word," from
Luke 1:38. As Kreeft explains,

> They are opposite sides of the same coin: Mary consented
> to carry the Savior of the whole world, the Christ, to birth,
> to life; and Frodo consented to carry the destroyer of the
> whole world, the Ring, the Antichrist, to its death. Mary
> gave life to Life (Christ); Frodo gave death to Death (the
> Ring). (Kreeft 204)

In Richard Purtill's *J.R.R. Tolkien: Myth, Morality, and Religion*,
Frodo is also identified as a Christ figure:

> Christ in traditional Christian theology dies for all human
> beings individually; Frodo is willing to lay down his life for
> all those threatened by evil, but especially for his own folk
> and his own friends. Yet in many ways Frodo's journey to
> Mordor is an echo, conscious or unconscious on Tolkien's
> part, of Christ's journey to Golgotha. (Purtill 74)

Frodo's sufferings in Mordor include being stripped of his garments and beaten with a whip (LOTR 889), being pierced with
thorns (LOTR 896), bearing the weight of the ring as a terrible
burden (LOTR 916), staggering while bearing his burden (LOTR
918). Frodo "stumbled" and "fell" (LOTR 919), then finally col-
lapsed. Sam, taking the role of Simon of Cyrene bearing the cross,
proclaims, "I can't carry it for you, but I can carry you and it as
well." Sam then carries Frodo and the Ring upon his back in one of

the novel's (and the 2003 film's) most emotional moments. Richard Purtill compared Frodo's "Passion" to the Five Sorrowful Mysteries of the Rosary: (1) the Agony in the Garden of Gethsemane, (2) Christ's Scourging at the Pillar, (3) the Crowning with Thorns, (4) the Carrying of the Cross, and (5) and Christ's Crucifixion and Death. Frodo's "death" in my analysis is in the moment he succumbs to the power of the Ring and fails to complete his mission. This moment, like Christ's death on Good Friday, seems to be Evil's moment of triumph.

Richard Purtill also sees Gandalf as Christ-like when he gives up his life for his friends on the bridge of Khazad-dum. (Purtill 118) In *The Power of the Ring: The Spiritual Vision Behind the Lord of the Rings* by Stratford Caldecott, Aragorn is viewed as a "type or prefigurement" of Jesus as Christ the King. (Caldecott 39) Peter Kreeft identified Gandalf, Frodo, and Aragorn as Christ figures because they all undergo different forms of death and resurrection. (Kreeft 222)

Gandalf the Grey sacrifices himself to save the Fellowship of the Ring in Moria, then returns as Gandalf the White. When he returns, Aragorn, Legolas, and Gimli do not recognize him (LOTR 481-483), just as Mary Magdalen didn't recognize Christ immediately after he rose from the tomb. (John 20: 11-18). His hair is described as "white as snow," his robe as "gleaming white," and his eyes as "piercing as the rays of the sun." (LOTR 483-484). Gandalf's appearance was so radiant that Gimli "sank to his knees, shading his eyes" (LOTR 484). Tolkien's language was chosen carefully to remind the reader of the appearance of Christ at the Transfiguration (Matthew 17:2) and also of the appearance of the angel of the Resurrection: "His appearance was like lightning and his garments white as snow." (Matthew 28:3, NRSV) Compare Gandalf the Grey's death experience with Harry's "death" and notice the similarities.

> "I threw down my enemy, and he fell from the high place and broke the mountainside where he smote it in his ruin. Then darkness took me, and I strayed out of thought and time, and I wandered far on roads that I will not tell." (LOTR 491)

Gandalf went on to explain how he returned to life as Gandalf the White: "Naked I was sent back—for a brief time, until my task is done. And naked I lay upon the mountain-top." (LOTR 491) He returned, but not as Gandalf the Grey: "Healing I found, and I was clothed in white." (LOTR 49) Compare this with Harry's "death and resurrection" experience:

> …it came to him that he must exist, must be more than dis-embodied thought, because he was lying, definitely lying, on some surface. Therefore he had a sense of touch, and the thing against which he lay existed too.
> Almost as soon as he had reached this conclusion, Harry became conscious that he was naked. (DH 705)

Harry, of course, wished for robes, and they appeared. Both Gandalf and Harry's nakedness may refer to Christ's nakedness upon the Cross, as well as this passage from Job 1:21, "Naked I come from the womb, naked shall I return to whence I came." J. R. R. Tolkien would have been very familiar with this passage. He was one of the translators for *The Jerusalem Bible*'s Book of Job.

Aragorn must walk the Paths of the Dead and liberate the souls in bondage he meets there before he can help win the Battle of Pelennor Fields and later claim his throne. Aragorn's healing gift also reveals his identity: *"The hands of the king are the hands of a healer."* His kingship is revealed when he heals Faramir, Eowyn, and Merry after the battle. Even the title of the third novel of *The Lord of the Rings* trilogy, named by the publisher as *The Return of the King*, the Second Coming of Christ is subtly suggested.

In Kreeft's analysis, the threefold nature of the Messiah as Prophet, Priest, and King is represented as follows: Gandalf as Prophet, the head; Frodo as Priest, the heart; and Aragorn as King, or hands. Kreeft explains that these three characters correspond to the three human powers of the soul: head, heart, and hands, or mind, emotions, and will. The "soul triptych" in *Harry Potter* was first identified in John Granger's writings. He has identified Harry as the spirit, Hermione as the mind, and Ron as the will. (Granger 119) The objects they receive in Dumbledore's last will and testament reinforce this interpretation. Harry, the "spirit", received the Golden Snitch/Resurrection Stone, which allowed him a brief reunion with the spirits of his beloved dead. Hermione, the "mind" of the trio, received a book, *The Tales of Beedle the Bard*, and within it, the mystery of the Deathly Hallows symbol left for her to solve. And finally, Ron, the "will" of the three heroes, received the Deluminator, which helped him to rescue and be reunited with his friends.

C.S. Lewis created one of the most beloved Christ figures in all of fantasy literature in the *Chronicles of Narnia*. In *The Lion, the Witch, and the Wardrobe*, Aslan, the golden lion, dies for the sins of the traitor, Edmund. He is stripped of his garments (his beautiful mane), mocked, jeered at, and then slaughtered like a sacrificial animal. Aslan's shocking and glorious resurrection leads to his defeat of the White Witch and the revival (resurrection) of all the creatures she has turned to stone. The triumph of Aslan is due to what Lewis calls "Deeper Magic from Before the Dawn of Time." J.K.

Rowling knows this Deeper Magic, and has made Harry walk the path that Frodo, Gandalf, and Aslan have walked before him.

Rowling gave her readers clues that Harry would wear the mantle of a Christ figure from the very beginning of his story. In *Harry Potter and the Sorcerer's Stone,* we learn that Voldemort tried to kill Harry in infancy, just as King Herod tried to kill the infant Jesus by ordering the slaughter of the innocents. After Harry prevented Quirrel's theft of the Philosopher's Stone, he remained unconscious in the hospital wing for three days. As in Frodo's story, the three days are reminiscent of the three days the body of Jesus Christ lay in the tomb before the resurrection. Jesus was crucified at the age of 33, and similarly, Frodo's involvement with the Ring began on his thirty-third birthday. Although Harry's adventures begin with the passing of his eleventh birthday, we must remember that he is a member of a trio of protagonists. Harry, Ron, and Hermione all board the Hogwarts express for the first time at the age of eleven: 11 multiplied by 3 yields the product of 33.

Jesus had the close friendship of Peter, James, and John who were from among his larger group of twelve apostles. In addition to the twelve, there were hundreds of disciples who followed him. Frodo was first accompanied on his long journey by his closest friends: Sam, Merry, and Pippin. Frodo's quest eventually attracted like-minded heroes who wanted to help him achieve his goal. The four hobbits, Gandalf, Aragorn, Legolas, Gimli and Boromir became the nine members of the Fellowship of the Ring. Eventually, thousands of troops from Rohan and Gondor fought against Sauron's forces in the War of the Ring. Harry's close friendship with Ron and Hermione expands to include Neville Longbottom, Ginny Weasley, and Luna Lovegood. These six friends became the most influential members of Dumbledore's Army. In addition to this student group, Harry's allies include other students from

Gryffindor, Ravenclaw, and Hufflepuff (and even a few Slytherins!) who would fight to defend the school. Harry's adult allies include the Order of the Phoenix, most of his teachers, and many others in the wizarding world who believe that Harry is the "Chosen One." The fact that Harry is thought to be the chosen one destined to fulfill the prophecy of Voldemort's demise also has a messianic overtone.

Jesus spent forty days in the wilderness and was tempted by Satan in the desert. Frodo spent most of his adventure wandering through the wilds of Middle-earth under the constant influence and temptation of Sauron's Ring. Harry faced temptation from Quirrell/Voldemort in book one, an attempted possession by Voldemort in book five, and the temptation of the locket Horcrux in book seven. Harry, Ron, and Hermione also made a long journey through the wilderness on their quest to defeat Voldemort.

In *Harry Potter and the Deathly Hallows*, Harry displays Christ-like qualities: He is quick to forgive Ron for abandoning the quest. He shows mercy towards his enemy Draco Malfoy and even saves his life twice. He forgives Severus Snape for his malice and cruelty. Harry also shows compassion for those traditionally unloved and disregarded in the wizarding world, such as house-elves, goblins, and muggle-borns. Indeed, many beings who were separated by their diversity were united by joining with Harry and his friends in their war against the forces of evil: "All were jumbled together, teachers and pupils, ghosts and parents, centaurs and house-elves." (DH 745) The same theme of diverse beings united as one people can also be found in the tales of Narnia and Middle-Earth. Christianity unites diversity in equality, as St. Paul says in Galatians 3:28 (NRSV), "There is no longer Jew or Greek, there is no longer slave or free, there is no longer male and female; for all of you are one in Christ Jesus."

Rowling has emphasized the need for equality and the evils of bigotry throughout the entire series of novels. Rowling often speaks through the words and actions of her characters. In *Harry Potter and the Deathly Hallows*, she speaks through Kingsley Shacklebolt:

> "I'd say that it's one short step from 'Wizards first' to 'Purebloods first' and then to 'Death Eaters'" replied Kingsley. "We're all human, aren't we? Every human life is worth the same, and worth saving." (DH 440)

Remus Lupin speaks for Rowling to illustrate how Harry (like Christ) is a symbol of hope in the darkest of times, even when the struggle against evil seems futile:

> "'The Boy Who Lived' remains a symbol of everything for which we are fighting: the triumph of good, the power of innocence, the need to keep resisting." (DH 441)

Harry, Ron, and Hermione hear these powerful words from Kingsley Shacklebolt and Remus Lupin on *Potterwatch*, a program broadcast over the Wizarding Wireless Network by the Order of the Phoenix. The program ends with these words of hope: "Keep each other safe. Keep faith. Good night." (DH 444)

Another parallel between Harry and Jesus is in that the Zealots of the time of Christ expected a messiah who would overthrow the Romans (Acts 1: 6-9), and likewise the members of Dumbledore's Army expected Harry to overthrow the Death Eaters who have taken over the Hogwarts school. Harry, like Jesus, knew that victory cannot be achieved by force.

Christ's wounds in the hands, feet, side, and head left him scarred. Both Frodo and Harry are wounded or scarred as well: Frodo has a

Nazgul-inflicted scar on his shoulder that will not completely heal, and a wound in the hand, his missing finger. Harry has a scar on his forehead that causes him pain when Voldemort feels strong emotions. He also has a scar on the back of his hand caused by the blood drawn from Umbridge's quill. His hand is marked with the words "I must not tell lies" from a punishment inflicted upon him two years prior to the events of the final novel.

In chapter 34 of the *Deathly Hallows*, Harry's walk through the Forbidden Forest to be handed over to Voldemort is similar to Christ's walk along the *Via Dolorosa* to Calvary. Harry has made the horrifying discovery that the snake Nagini isn't the only Horcrux that remains. Voldemort's soul was torn by the murder of James and Lily Potter, and as a result of the Dark Lord's killing curse being made ineffectual by Lily's self-sacrifice, a fragment of Voldemort's soul is trapped within Harry's own body. In order to destroy this living Horcrux, Harry must allow himself to be killed. He bravely faces his own death, hoping that Voldemort will be defeated by someone else when he becomes mortal again.

The parallels between Christ and Harry Potter in this chapter are numerous. Jesus, the sacrificial Lamb of God, went willingly to his death in obedience to the Father's will. The image of Harry as a sacrificial animal is present in the narrative when Snape says in disgust that Harry has been "raised like a pig for slaughter." (DH 687) Jesus was tempted in the Garden of Gethsemane to ask the Father to spare him from death on the cross: "…let this cup pass from me." (Matt. 26:39, NRSV) Christ overcame this temptation and completed the task given to him by God the Father. In the seventh book Harry was tempted to seek power for himself (the Hallows) rather than fulfill the mission Dumbledore sent him on, the mission to destroy the Horcruxes. Harry, like Jesus, had to choose between saving himself from death or saving the world from the triumph of evil. Harry, like Christ, chose to give up his life for the sake of those he loves. Jesus had a crisis of faith on the cross: "My God, my God, why have you forsaken me?" (Matt. 27:46, NRSV) Harry had a crisis of faith in Dumbledore throughout the seventh book because of Rita Skeeter's lies and the rumors he heard about Dumbledore's past. He felt abandoned by Dumbledore because the old wizard died and left Harry, Ron, and Hermione with a seemingly impossible task to complete and little information on how to do it. In the Garden of Gethsemane, Jesus took Peter, James, and John with him to pray. In chapter 34, Harry used the Resurrection Stone to see his beloved dead. He was accompanied on his walk through the forest by *James* Potter, Remus *John* Lupin, and Sirius Black. Just as Jesus' mother Mary was present on the way to Calvary and at the Crucifixion, the soul of Harry's mother Lily was with her son on his walk through the forest. In Christian symbolism the lily is both a symbol of the Blessed Virgin Mary and of Easter, the holy day on which Christians celebrate Christ's Resurrection.

Just as Christ obeyed the Father's will and died a sacrificial death, so did Harry obey Dumbledore's will and give himself over to be killed by Voldemort in order to destroy the Horcrux that Harry had become. Christ's obedience led him to the *cross* where he was proclaimed *King* of the Jews. Harry's obedience to the will of Albus Dumbledore led him to *King's Cross*, where he discovered the fate of Voldemort's soul fragment, now removed permanently from Harry's body.

Near-sighted Harry Potter had worn glasses for most of his life, but while in "King's Cross" he discovered he didn't need them. His vision is perfect. Harry had a scar that he received in fifth year from his detentions with Dolores Umbridge, but when he looks on the back of his hand, it is no longer there. Harry's body is his own, but without imperfections. In Christianity, the faithful believe in the resurrection of the body. This means that the soul receives a glorified resurrection body which is freed from all forms of disease and is devoid of any flaws. During the time spent in the limbo of "King's Cross" Harry has to make a decision: should he board a train and go on to his "next great adventure" or should he return to his friends who are still fighting the war against evil? Harry decides to go back to his friends, to the world of the living.

The art for chapter 36 "The Flaw in the Plan" in the American edition of *DH* shows a weeping Hagrid carrying Harry's (presumably) dead body. Hagrid, although strong and masculine, has nurturing, motherly qualities: he bakes cakes, serves tea, even wears an apron. He likes to play "mummy" to a variety of dangerous creatures such as Norbert the Dragon or his giant baby brother Grawp. This image of the weeping Hagrid is reminiscent of the image of the *Mater Dolorosa* or "Sorrowful Mother" of Michelangelo's *Pieta*. The imagery of the *Pieta* is also present in the film version of *Harry Potter and the Order of the Phoenix* when Dumbledore is shown holding Harry's unconscious body after the battle in the Ministry of Magic. Harry's love for his friends and family is vividly portrayed in the film as the powerful force that prevents Voldemort from possessing Harry. This emotional scene ends with Dumbledore cradling Harry's seemingly lifeless, unconscious body in his arms, foreshadowing Harry's apparent "death" in Book Seven.

Romans 6:23 describes the wages of sin as *death*. Just as Christ's death on the cross saves Christians from the "wages of sin," so does Harry's willingness to sacrifice himself offer a magical protection to all those who are fighting on the side of good at the Battle of Hogwarts. The curses of Voldemort and his Death Eaters have no effect on the defenders of Hogwarts, and *none of the beings fighting on the side of good will die from this point in the story onward.* "The last enemy to be destroyed is *death*." (Cor. 15:26)

THE LORD OF THE HALLOWS

Jesus defeated death by the ultimate act of love: self-sacrifice. Harry's willingness to die to save his friends is what defeats Voldemort as well. The Gospel of John describes the sacrifice of Jesus Christ in a manner which also describes the heroism of Harry Potter: "Greater love hath no one than this, that a man lay down his life for his friends." (John 15:13, KJV)

In Harry's visit to the "limbo" that resembles King's Cross Station, he sees what will happen to Voldemort if he dies *unrepentant*. Dumbledore tells Harry that in the afterlife "there is no help possible" for Voldemort if he dies without feeling *remorse* for what he has done. This interlude presents a view of Hell for the unrepentant which is an eternal separation from God. Those who are sent there cry out for help, but like the pitiful crying thing that Harry doesn't want to look at when he is at "King's Cross," the cries of those eternally separated from God will not be answered.

Chapter 36 "The Flaw in the Plan" is rich in Christian imagery and meaning. When Narcissa Malfoy announces "He is dead!" the Death Eaters yell in triumph and stomp their feet, as all of the minions of Hell must have rejoiced at the death of Christ. Just as Jesus' body was mocked and spit upon by non-believers at the crucifixion, Harry's body (assumed to be dead) is *crucioed* by Voldemort three times. The name of the *Cruciatus* curse is here to remind us once again of the crucifixion. The sorrow of Jesus' loved ones, his mother Mary, John, and Mary Magdalen who were eyewitnesses to Christ's torture and death upon the cross, also has a parallel in the sorrow of Harry's loved ones, among them are Hermione, Ron, and Ginny who were also eyewitnesses to Harry's degradation after his apparent death.

Nagini the snake is the only Horcrux that remained. The serpent as a symbol of Satan is used throughout scripture, beginning with Genesis 3:15, the prophecy of the woman (Eve) and the serpent

FRODO AND HARRY AS CHRIST FIGURES

(Satan): "I will put enmity between you and the woman, and between your offspring and hers; he *will strike your head*, and you will strike his heel." (NRSV) In C.S. Lewis' *The Silver Chair*, the Lady of the Green Kirtle is an evil witch who can transform herself into a serpent. At the climax of the novel, Prince Rillian, a "Son of Adam" uses his sword to strike at the head of the serpent in order to decapitate her. In *Deathly Hallows*, it is also a "Son of Adam," Neville Longbottom, who strikes at the head of the serpent: Neville uses Godric Gryffindor's sword to strike at the head of Nagini. Neville decapitates the snake, destroying the last Horcrux. Voldemort is motal again.

11

The Long Defeat and Glimpses of Final Victory

"...together through ages of the world we have fought the long defeat."—Galadriel in *The Lord of the Rings*

"...for Wars are always lost, and the War always goes on..."—J.R.R. Tolkien, June 3, 1945

"War is always a defeat for humanity."—Pope John Paul II, January 13, 2003

"Evil is immortal. All our victories against it in this world are temporary."—Peter Kreeft

In *The Lord of the Rings* Tolkien presented his readers a theological worldview that illustrated the might and indestructibility of evil. Though the heroes of the War of the Ring stood in opposition to the forces of Sauron, and even won a great battle against their adversary, ultimately evil could not be defeated by force of arms. Gandalf, wisest of wizards knew this to be true:

"I am Gandalf, Gandalf the White, but Black is mightier
still." (LOTR 489)

"My lords, listen to the words of the Steward of Gondor
before he died: '*You may triumph on the fields of Pelennor for a
day, but against the Power that has now arisen there is no victory.*' I
do not bid you to despair, as he did, but to ponder the truth
in these words." (LOTR 860)

"Other evils there are that may come, for Sauron is himself
but a servant or emissary." (LOTR 861)

Tolkien gave an explanation of the immortal, indestructible nature of evil in a letter he wrote, dated December 15, 1956:

"Actually I am a Christian, and indeed a Roman Catholic,
so that I do not expect 'history' to be anything but a 'long
defeat'—though it contains (and in a legend, may contain
more clearly and movingly) some samples or glimpses of
final victory." (*Letters* 255)

From these quotations, we have a clear notion of what Tolkien
thought about the nature of evil and the futility of war, but would
Rowling agree with Tolkien's philosophy? How are we to deal with
such an indestructible, overpowering evil in our lifetimes? Tolkien
commented on this in another letter:

"…it is not for us to choose the times into which we are
born, but to do what we could to repair them; but the spirit
of wickedness in high places is now so powerful and so
many-headed in its incarnations that there seems nothing
more to do than personally refuse to worship any of the
hydras' heads…" (*Letters* 402)

Rowling used the exact same image of the many-headed hydra as a symbol of the immortality of evil. In this passage, Severus Snape showed his keen understanding of the nature of the Powers of Darkness, an understanding he has gained because he once served those powers:

> "The Dark Arts," said Snape, "are many, varied, ever-changing, and eternal. Fighting them is like fighting a many-headed monster which each time a neck is severed, sprouts a head even fiercer and cleverer than before. You are fighting that which is unfixed, mutating, and indestructible." (HBP 177)

Yet as Rowling later reminds us, we must (like St. Paul), "fight the good fight."

> It was important, Dumbledore said, to fight, and fight again, and keep fighting, for only then could evil be kept at bay, though never quite eradicated. (HBP 644-645)

But if evil cannot ever truly be defeated, how does the hero triumph? If he cannot win by force of arms, should the hero just surrender? For most of us, the answer is *no*. We must continue not to worship any of the hydra's heads, and to fight the good fight. But for Harry, like Jesus, the answer is *yes*. He must surrender; he must give up his life.

Evil only understands power, as when Voldemort proclaims, "There is no good and evil, there is only power, and those too weak to seek it." (SS 291) Evil understands power, but not weakness; pride, but not humility; selfishness, but not selflessness. In an act of spiritual judo, Jesus turned the strength of evil against itself. By allowing himself to be crucified, he rose triumphant over sin. Through his resurrection he conquered death. In summary, the hero does not defeat evil, but he helps it to defeat itself. This is the essence of Christ's victory over Satan at Calvary. Harry's triumph over Voldemort in "legend" (as Tolkien would call it), is one of the "glimpses of final victory" in the eternal struggle against evil.

The word *eucatastrophe* was coined by J.R.R. Tolkien to refer to the sudden turn of events at the end of a story which transform a catastrophic event into a triumph of goodness. He used the word to describe the destruction of the One Ring and the defeat of Sauron at the end of *The Lord of the Rings*. In his essay "On Fairy Stories" Tolkien explains that the eucatastrophe found in fairy tales has entered our world as well. "The Birth of Christ is the eucatastrophe of Man's history. The Resurrection is the eucatastrophe of the story of the Incarnation. This story begins and ends in joy." (*Tolkien Reader* 88-89) After all of the death and suffering Harry has witnessed in his young life, the reader takes comfort in the fact that the story of The Boy Who Lived also begins and ends in joy.

Harry hid beneath the Invisibility Cloak in the chaos of the battle that followed Neville's triumph over the serpent. When Harry finally pulled off the cloak to reveal his presence, there were triumphant cries of "HE'S ALIVE!" When confronted by Voldemort, the man who tried to kill him so many times, Harry showed compassion for his worst enemy, his parents' murderer. He had seen what Voldemort would become in the next life, and tried to save him.

> "I'd advise you to think about what you've done…Think and try some remorse, Riddle […] It's your one chance. It's all you've got left…I've seen what you'll be otherwise…Be a man… try…Try for some remorse." (DH 741)

THE LONG DEFEAT AND GLIMPSES OF FINAL VICTORY

Just after the release of *Harry Potter and the Deathly Hallows*, Rowling explained that if Voldemort "could have mustered the courage to repent, he would have been okay. But, of course, he wouldn't. And that was his choice." (Dateline MSNBC July 30, 2007) Her use of the word "repent" is very significant. In Christianity, true repentance is the only way one can obtain salvation for one's sins.

Voldemort remained unrepentant until the end and tried to curse Harry with Avada Kedavra, the death curse. Harry's only defense was Expelliarmus: the disarming spell. Voldemort died when his own death curse backfired on him. What followed was a moment of absolute joy as Harry was embraced by his friends and loved ones.

> The consolation of fairy-stories is the joy of the happy ending: or more correctly of the good catastrophe, the sudden joyous "turn"...It does not deny the existence of dyscatastrophe, of sorrow and failure: the possiblilty of these is necessary to the joy of deliverance; it denies...universal final defeat...giving a fleeting glimpse of joy. Joy beyond the walls of the world, poignant as grief. (*Tolkien Reader* 85-86)

Harry, joyfully reunited with his loved ones, goes on to live a full life, renouncing the power of the Elder Wand, and becoming a true Master of Death. In Tolkien's essay, "On Fairy Stories" he explained that the fairy story allows us to experience the fulfillment of humanity's oldest and deepest desire, "the Great Escape, the Escape from Death." Rowling teaches us that we cannot escape from Death, but we can conquer it by embracing it, accepting the fact that we all must die. Death is not the end of our existence; it is only the beginning. Our souls are eternal. We all have the Power the

Dark Lord Know Not: *love,* the only power that transcends death.

As Dumbledore told Harry, "The true master does not seek to run away from Death. He accepts that he must die, and understands that there are far, far worse things in the living world than dying." (DH 720-721) A life lived without love is one of them.

In Conclusion

What is the secret of the success of the Harry Potter novels? Could the popularity of these books be due to the fact that Harry's story resonates with an older, more powerful story?

During a press conference in October 2007, which followed the release of the final novel, Rowling said, "To me [the religious parallels have] always been obvious. But I never wanted to talk too openly about it because I thought it might show people who just wanted the story where we were going." (Adler 1) With regards to the two Biblical quotations, Matthew 6:19 and 1 Corinthians 15:26, Rowling said, "They're very British books, so on a very practical note Harry was going to find Biblical quotations on tombstones, but I think those two particular quotations he finds on the tombstones at Godric's Hollow, they sum up—they almost epitomize the whole series." (Adler 2)

Perhaps J. K. Rowling has done what C. S. Lewis and J. R. R. Tolkien have already done before her: smuggled the Gospel past the watchful dragons of our time in the form of a Christian story disguised as a fantasy adventure. Any skeptical dragon of this post-Christian age will, of course, try to deny the reality of the true Lord of the Hallows. They do not recognize Him when he appears in disguise in the pages of a modern day fairy story, for after all, "of house elves and children's tales, of love, loyalty, and innocence Voldemort knows and understands nothing." (DH 709) The watchful dragons of secularism that C. S. Lewis described have been asleep, and may they continue to slumber as J. K. Rowling's tale of courage, friendship, and love is smuggled into the households and libraries of our fallen world. Rowling, in her wisdom and cleverness, has given us excellent advice to follow in the Hogwarts School Motto: "Draco Dormiens Nunquam Titillandus": "Never Tickle a Sleeping Dragon!"

Works Cited

"About the Books: transcript of J. K. Rowling's live interview on Scholastic.com," Scholastic.com, 16 October 2000 <http://www.accio-quote.org/articles/2000/1000-scholastic-chat.htm>

Adler, Shawn. "Harry Potter Author J. K. Rowling Opens Up About Books' Christian Imagery." MTV.com 17 October 2007 <http://www.accio-quote.org/articles/2007/1017.mtv-adler.html>

Anelli, Melissa and Emerson Spartz. "The Leaky Cauldron/MuggleNet interview" The Leaky Cauldron, 16 July 2005. <http://www.accio-quote.org/articles/2005/0705-tlc_mugglenet-anelli-1.htm>,<http://www.accio-quote.org/articles/2005/0705-tlc_mugglenet-anelli-2.htm>,<http://www.accio-quote.org/articles/2005/0705-tlc_mugglenet-anelli-3.htm>

Apostolos-Cappadona, Diane. *Dictionary of Christian Art.* New York: Continuum, 1994.

Barnes&Noblechattranscript,Barnes&Noble.com,8September 1999 <http://www.accio-quote.org/articles/1999/0999-barnesnoble-staff.htm>

Biedermann, Hans. Trans. James Hulbert. *Dictionary of Symbolism.* New York: Meridian, 1994.

Birmingham, Carrie. "Harry Potter and the Baptism of the Imagination." <http://www.zossima.com>

Bradner, John. *Symbols of Church Seasons and Days.* Harrisburg: Morehouse, 1977.

Bunson, Matthew, Margaret Bunson, Stephen Bunson. *Our Sunday Visitor's Encyclopedia of Saints.* Our Sunday Visitor's Publishing Division, 2003.

Caldecott, Stratford. *The Power of the Ring: The Spiritual Vision Behind the Lord of the Rings.* New York: Crossroad, 2005.

Cavallo, Adolfo Salvatore. *The Unicorn Tapestries.* New York: Harry N. Abrams, 1998.

Charbonneau-Lassay, Louis. *The Bestiary of Christ.* New York: Penguin, 1992.

Colbert, David. *The Magical Worlds of Harry Potter.* New York: Penguin, 2001.

___. *The Magical Worlds of Harry Potter.* 2nd ed. New York: Penguin, 2004.

___. *The Magical Worlds of Narnia.* New York: Penguin, 2005.

Delahoyde, Michael. "Medieval Art: The Unicorn Tapestries." <http://www.wsu.edu/~delahoyd/medieval/unicorn/.html>

DeBertodano, Helena. "Harry Potter Charms a Nation." *Electronic Telegraph.* 25 July 1998. <http://www.accio-quote.org/articles/1998/0798-telegraph-bertodano.html>

Ellwood, W. *Saints, Signs, and Symbols.* Harrisburg, PA: Morehouse, 1974.

Ferguson, George. *Signs and Symbols in Christian Art.* New York: Oxford UP, 1961.

Gibson, Clare. *The Hidden Life of Renaissance Art: Secrets and Symbols in Great Masterpieces.* New York: Barnes & Noble, 2007.

Granger, John. *The Hidden Key to Harry Potter.* Hadlock, WA: Zossima, 2002.

WORKS CITED

Griffin, Justin. *The Grail Procession.* Jefferson, NC: McFarland, 2004.

____.*The Holy Grail: The Legend, the History, the Evidence.* Jefferson, NC: McFarland, 2001.

Gulevich, Tanya. *The Encyclopedia of Christmas.* Detroit, MI: Omnigraphics, 2000.

Hall, James. *Dictionary of Subjects and Symbols in Art.* New York: Harper and Row, 1979.

Harry Potter and the Order of the Phoenix. Dir. David Yates. Perf. Michael Gambon and Daniel Radcliffe. Warner Brothers, 2007.

Jurgens, William A., ed. *The Faith of the Early Church Fathers.* Vol. 1, Collegeville, MN: The Liturgical Press, 1970. 3 vols.

King, Larry. "J. K. Rowling Discusses the Surprising Success of 'Harry Potter'," Larry King Live (CNN), 20 October 2000 <http://transcripts.cnn.com/TRANSCRIPTS/0010/20/lkl.00.html>

Kreeft, Peter J. *Catholic Christianity.* San Francisco: Ignatius, 2001.

____.*The Philosophy of Tolkien: The Worldview Behind* The Lord of the Rings. San Francisco: Ignatius, 2005.

Lewis, C. S. *The Chronicles of Narnia.* New York: Harper Collins, 1950-1956.

____. "Sometimes Fairy Stories May Say Best What's to Be Said." *On Stories.* San Diego: Harcourt, 1982.

Lewis, Warren H., ed. *The Letters of C. S. Lewis.* New York: Harcourt, Brace & World, 1966.

Lydon, Christopher. J. K. Rowling interview transcript. *The Connection.* (WBWR Radio) 12 October 1999 <http://www.accio-quote.org/articles/1999/1099-connectiontransc2.htm>

Matarasso, P. M., *The Quest for the Holy Grail.* London: Penguin, 1969.

Matthews, John. *The Grail:Quest for the Eternal.* London: Thames and Hudson, 1981.

McIntosh, Kenneth. *The Grail, the Shroud, and Other Religious Relics.* Philadelphia, PA: Moon Crest Publishers, 2006.

Morgan, Giles. *The Holy Grail.* NJ: Chartwell Books, 2006.

Murphy, G. Ronald. *Gemstone of Paradise: The Holy Grail in Wolfram's Parzival.* Oxford: Oxford UP, 2006.

Nicol, Patricia. "Boy wizard frees trapped mother" *Sunday Times* (London) 6 December 1998. <http://www.accio-quote.org/articles/198/1298-sundaytimes-nicol.html>

Pearce, Joseph. *Tolkien: Man and Myth.* San Francisco: Ignatius Press, 1998. Post,

Purtill, Richard. *J.R.R. Tolkien: Myth, Morality, and Religion.* San Francisco: Ignatius, 2003.

Rowling, J. K. *Fantastic Beasts and Where to Find Them.* New-York: Levine-Scholastic, 2001.

____. *Harry Potter and the Chamber of Secrets.* New York: Levine-Scholastic, 1999.

____. *Harry Potter and the Deathly Hallows.* New York: Levine-Scholastic, 2007.

____. *Harry Potter and the Goblet of Fire.* New York: Levine-Scholastic, 2000.

____. *Harry Potter and the Half-Blood Prince.* New York: Levine-Scholastic, 2005.

____. *Harry Potter and the Order of the Phoenix.* New York: Levine-Scholastic, 2003.

____. *Harry Potter and the Prisoner of Azkaban.* New York: Levine-Scholastic, 1999.

____. *Harry Potter and the Sorcerer's Stone.* New York: Levine-Scholastic, 1998.

____. J. K. Rowling Official Site. "J. K. Rowling at the Edinburgh

WORKS CITED

Book Festival." 15 August 2004. <http://www.jkrowling.com/textonly/en/news_view.cfm?id=80>

___. "El Pais Interview." 8 February 2008. <http://www.accio-quote.org/articles/list2008.html>

___. "Red Nose Day Chat." *BBC Online* 12 March 2001. <http://www.accio-quote.org/articles/list2008.html>

___. *The Tales of Beedle the Bard.* New York: Levine-Scholastic, 2008.

Sidi, Smadar Shir. *The Complete Book of Hebrew Baby Names.* San Francisco: Harper Collins, 1989.

Solomon, Evan. "J. K. Rowling Interview." *CBC Newsround* 2000 <http://www.accio-quote.org/Articles/2000/0700-hottype-solomon.htm>

Tolkien, J. R. R. *The Letters of J. R. R. Tolkien.* Ed. Humphrey Carpenter. New York: Houghton Mifflin, 1981, 2000.

Tolkien, J. R. R. *The Hobbit.* New York: Houghton Mifflin, 1937, 1997.

___. *The Lord of the Rings.* New York: Houghton Mifflin, 1954-55, 1994.

___. "On Fairy Stories." *The Tolkien Reader.* New York: Ballantine Books, 1966.

Vieira, Meredith. "Harry Potter: The Final Chapter," MSNBC Dateline, 30 July 2007. <http://www.accio-quote.org/articles/2007/0726-today-vieira1.html> <http://www.accio-quote.org/articles/2007/0726-today-vieira2.html>

Von Eschenbach, Wolfram. *Parzival.* Trans. A. T. Hatto. New York: Penguin Books, 1980.

Wyman, Max. "You Can Lead a Fool to a Book but You Can't Make Them Think: Author Has Frank Words for the Religious Right." *Vancouver Sun.* 26 October 2000.

CPSIA information can be obtained at www.ICGtesting.com
Printed in the USA
BVOW03s0957271014

372493BV00008B/237/P

9 781432 741129